BOUND BY OBSESSION

DELIA BRAUN

CONTENTS

CHAPTER 1

"I know that we don't know each other that well, and it's absolutely my fault. However, I would like us to get to know each other better and form a relationship. I can imagine that you're going through a lot after your mother's passing, and I just don't want you to do this alone. So, I would love for you to move in with me and my family, and I can try as best as I can to be there for you. If you would like, of course."

I didn't know my father all that well, or at all for that matter. My mother didn't go out of her way to tell me about him, and I didn't really bother to ask because I figured that if he wanted to be in my life then he would be, and since he wasn't, I took the rejection with a pinch of salt and lived my life. I grew up in a two bedroom flat in the more run down parts of Johannesburg, while my mother worked a job in retail and my grandmother stayed home to take care of me.

I wouldn't say that life was all that glamorous because there were moments when things got financially difficult for my mother, but I can guarantee that we were happy. My mother was my best friend, since there was only a 17 year gap between us, we were like friends more than we were like mother and daughter. And she liked to be young, or more like, liked to act young with her crop tops and cleavage, booty shorts and tattoos on her dark skin. She would wear bright lipstick and hoop earrings, date men with beat up cars who were no good and were usually married. She would party every weekend at shebeens and the hookah pipe was practically her wind pipe.

She was honestly just a woman who lived her life to the fullest and I couldn't blame her or stop her because I loved watching her live her life, although, I could have missed out on those moments when I would come home on a random weekday to find her passed out on the couch with several empty bottles of beer surrounding her body.

I couldn't complain though because she provided for me. I had everything that I wanted. If I wanted a new shoe that just came out, she would get it for me, if I needed new clothes for whatever reason that I came up with, she would get it for me, if I wanted extra allowance, she made sure that I got it. I never felt like I didn't fit in because I always had what others had around me.

On a random Thursday afternoon, my mother suddenly collapsed in the middle of the kitchen and when we rushed to the hospital we found out that her organs were failing and it was only minutes before we would have to say our final goodbyes. After my mother took her final breath, I felt like I had nothing left to live for since my grandmother had passed on two years earlier. I wanted to follow behind my two favourite and only people in the world. So after my mum's funeral where distant relatives that I knew nothing about tried to comfort me only to leave me alone hours later, I stood in the kitchen with a rope hanging above me. Just as I stood on a crate to wrap the rope around my neck, with tears running down my face and a racing heart- my mother's ringtone blared loud and I looked at the foreign number flashing across the old and beaten Huawei screen. I contemplated carrying out my suicide or answering the call. After two more rings I found myself stepping down from the crate and placing the phone to my ear only to hear the male voice that belonged to my so called father.

Three days later I'm standing outside an American airport, looking at a man that was literally half of me. "Hi." He said with a shaky voice as if he was nervous to meet me. I looked at him as if he were some hallucination, blinking several times to make sure that it was him. He stood at a height of 5'11 and his hair was curly and long. His skin was beige and light and his eyes were amber coloured. I could tell that he was biracial and his features were good looking but older. He had a salt and pepper beard and he was wearing a big brown coat.

I stood there with my one suitcase in hand and a backpack strapped safely to my back. I don't know when I finally found my voice, "hi." My voice and accent was very different from his heavily American with another kind of accent that I couldn't exactly pinpoint just yet but would later find out to be Italian.

My eyes strayed from his and I looked around. The air felt different, the sky didn't look the same, and everything about this place was foreign. I didn't do too well with unfamiliar environments but what could I say? It's not like I had anything else going for me.

"Let me take that off your hands, and we can make our way home." he said to me as he took my suitcase and put it in the backseat of the blue Ford EcoSport before he opened the passenger door for me. I looked at him hesitantly, wondering if I should get inside the car because I had a sinking feeling in my stomach. But then again, if I didn't then where would I go? I chalked up the nerves to the change of environment and home sickness before I got into the car and he closed the door behind me.

I pulled my earphones out of my ears and looked outside the passenger window, taking everything in. I already missed home and the familiar sight of Quantum's and Siyaya's speeding by and swerving dangerously on the road. "how was your flight?" he asked me with his deep voice and I was still taken aback by it. I slightly jumped in my sear before I uncomfortably shifted in the seat as I put on my seatbelt.

I cleared my throat, "it was okay." I answered him as I began to fidget with my earphones. The flight had been more than okay, he had bought me first class tickets so I had flown all the way from South Africa in luxury. I had never been on a plane before and it was my first time and while I had been very nervous when I had been driven to the O.R. Tambo International Airport, the experience wasn't a bad one even though I got lost a few times.

"That's good." He said before we fell into an awkward silence. I bit my lower lip and looked outside the windshield to look at the road ahead, asking myself how in the hell I got here even though I knew how that happened. After a few moments I saw him reaching for the radio before soft music began to play through. "what sort of music do you like?" he asked me as he drummed his fingers on the steering wheel.

The true answer would have been either opera music or amapiano, but I didn't feel like saying anything to him so I simply shrugged. "I don't know." I responded in a distant tone as I listened to the song that he was playing at the moment.

"Well, this song is called Hearing Damage." He told me but I already knew the song.

Hello, I have hate watched twilight and this particular song was the one thing about the movie franchise that I actually enjoyed. Amongst the moments when Jacob Black would take off his shirt and flash his abs. "my daughter, Greta, is obsessed with this song." He continued to say and I only looked ahead, not responding to him as I continued to fidget with my earphones.

I wasn't entirely comfortable with him yet and I can't imagine that it will get easier since I am going to meet his family, and I'm going to hate how awkward that's possibly going to be. He must have gotten the hint that I wasn't in the mood to talk before he fell silent and let the music fill up the heavy silence in the car. My eyes followed the road to the horizon, looking at the orange sky as I thought of my mother and how our flat gave the best views of the sunset. I gripped onto the locket chain around my neck that had a picture of my mother and grandmother in it, holding it tightly as if it would somehow bring back the hands of time and I would suddenly wake up from this nightmare and find myself in my old bed.

...But that didn't happen.

CHAPTER 2

I let out a loud puff of air as I tucked my hands further into the pockets of my dad's beat up jacket that had obviously seen better days. I had thrown it on over my short shorts and crop top that I had been laying around in all day because I had nothing better to do. The jacket was big on my figure and reached just below my butt, covering the short shorts and making it seem as though I wasn't wearing anything underneath the jacket. I wore a pair of fluffy emoji slippers that my dad's wife, Gabriela had gifted me with on a random Monday afternoon. I had my hair in a high, neat and tight bun that made me look more than decent. My large framed polka dot glasses allowed me to see two feet ahead of me, and allowed me to look around the town that I was in.

I was running an arrand for my dad and Gabriela. They hadn't asked me to, but I had volunteered when they came knocking on my bedroom door that I happened to share with my ten year old and sixteen year old half-sisters, and said that they were going to get milk, bread and snacks from the gas station just down the road that had almost everything to offer. I was bored out of my mind from staying home and doing nothing that I jumped at the chance, because I remembered where the gas station was and it was no more than a five minute walk from the house.

My father lived in a town called Merton and he had revealed that it was an Italian town with mostly Italian residents and it was almost rare to come across someone who wasn't Italian in this town. I found out that my father's mother had been an Italian woman who happened to have a one night stand in Vegas with some random black man, and lo and behold, 9 months later my father popped out.

He was born and raised in Merton, and the one time that he decided to venture out and travel the world, he happened to arrive in Cape Town and when he did, he met a young 17 year old varsity student by the name of Miriam and they spent a few days together and he left, later on finding out that she had fallen pregnant but never getting the chance to meet his daughter except once every few years until things just regrettably died down and they lost touch. That is, of course, what he told me. My father was clearly not a fan of silence and whenever I was silent and wouldn't say anything, he wanted to fill the silence with whatever words that he could come up with.

His wife Gabriela was a dark haired Italian woman who was loud mouthed and talked a lot of shit about everyone else, and no doubt, probably myself behind my back since I was her husband's black child that appeared out of the blue and was now living with them. Her tanned skin and perfect looking mixed children were a sign that I was definitely the black sheep of the family. I can't really fault her because she has been accommo-dating and nice to me, however, if we could lay off the pasta a little bit, I probably would appreciate it a bit more but of course I'll keep those words to myself. I feared the woman loved pasta so much, she would end up becoming it.

Gabriela and my father, Alessandro had three children together. Two daughters and a son. Their oldest daughter was sixteen, and her name was Greta, then there came ten year old Aurora, and then their youngest, 6 year old Matteo.

"So, Delaney, are you excited to go to your job tomorrow?" my train of thought was interrupted by Greta and I looked at her, my eyes looking over her face as I took in her features one more time. She was beautiful, she had long slightly curly hair that reached the middle of her back and framed her like a mane. She had warm ivory toned skin and her eyes were a beautiful amber just like my fathers. Her lips were lightly pink and her cheeks slightly full. She stood at the same height as I did at 5'6 and she was quite talkative.

Gabriela and Alessandro had suggested that I go with Greta to the store since I was still new to Merton and I could get lost, and just to make sure that I was safe. I don't know if they expected me to just run away, even though there's no way in hell that I would since I had nowhere to go.

I shrugged in response to her question. Alessandro had managed to get a waitressing job at one of his friends restaurants and I wasn't all too excited about it but I was glad to do something that would get me out of that 3 bedroom 2 bathroom Italian style home. "I guess you could say that." I responded as I looked ahead of us, at the streets that were lit with high streetlights that made it look like it was day.

The streets were silent and each homes lights were on. There was the occasional dog howling and barking, cats meowing in the bushes on the other side of the road and the sound of distant music. Greta and I's footsteps synced and we walked with similar rhythm, it was almost impressive. I looked ahead at the gas station that we were fast approaching.

"Cool. Maybe you'll make enough money to save up for a car and you can give me rides to school or around town," she said with excitement as she peered into my eyes with a wide grin across her face. I almost loved how happy she was and how bright of a smile she had. I could tell that she had a good heart because of the way that she carried herself and the way that she treated me. Each time I looked into those amber coloured eyes I saw a young girl that had a father and mother, and had lost no one, and I was jealous of it as much as I loved that for her.

Even though I have only known her a week, we got along in the sense that she would talk my ear off and I would listen and respond every once in a while. She told me about her silly crushes, about boys at school who liked her and gave her gifts and letters on the daily, about the girls who didn't like her, about the nerds that she sat with instead of with her other friends, about the pet hamster that her class has and everything in between.

I gave her a small smile and nodded my head, "yes. Maybe we can do that." I wasn't too sure a waitressing pay check could get you a car but then again, you never know. But I do know that I would probably save up to get my own place or I'll end up being the 40 year old half sister who still lives with the parents.

I pushed open the doors of the gas station store and a bell sounded over me, announcing my arrival. I was surprised by how large the store was and how much you could get. "come on, this way." Greta urged as she pulled on my arm and led me down to the particular items that we needed to get. After we had gotten the milk and bread, Greta told me with a grin that we could buy just one item that we could snack on, on the way home- before she beelined for the fridges while I walked down the aisle, looking for a familiar brand of crisps (chips).

As I was looking over all the different bags of crisp, I looked behind me, outside at the gas pumps where I saw a number of blacked out cars and men in suits filling up their cars. They had not been here before so they must have just arrived. I furrowed my eyebrows at how strange it was that so many blacked out BMW's were parked with men in black suits filling their tanks. My eye was caught by the packet of Doritos and just as I was about to grab it, I heard Greta call my name. "Delaney!" she called in a panicked whisper.

I quickly turned to see what the matter was to see her crouching and hiding behind the stack of items. She urgently motioned for me to get down and I frowned but did as she said, "what's wrong?" I asked her, wondering what this could be about.

"Don't let them see you." She said and as I looked into her eyes, I saw panic and worry.

"Who?" I asked in confusion, starting to become slightly cautious and afraid of possible dangers lurking especially since I was with my 16 year old half sister and we were both petite girls who wouldn't be ablet to put up much of a fight.

"The men outside. They're dangerous." She told me in a whisper as she looked all around us.

I heard the doors open and the bell chime and she placed her finger on her lips before she gripped my hand and motioned for me to get to the back of the store. I followed behind her, still crouched down as she led me to a corner where she managed to squeeze herself in and then force me to squeeze in there with her. I followed her instruction and just as I was about to talk, she slapped her hands over my mouth to stop me.

I saw how her eyes and face were covered in panic and decided to just sit still. There's nothing worse than not understanding whatever is going on.

Just moments after I heard the door open again and the bell chime. We continued to stay hidden for some time and when it had been over ten minutes, we finally got out, and when we stood to our feet, all the cars that once were there were gone. Greta gripped onto the milk and bread, "let's go home." she said to me as we walked to the register.

We found the young boy who was supposed to be standing behind the register, hiding. "they're gone, Lorenzo." Greta announced and the boy appeared from below the counter and looked at us. His face had worry across it before he looked outside and when he saw that the coast was clear he nodded at Greta and then rang up the items before taking the money that Greta offered.

Greta turned to look at me, "we need to run." She said to me as we approached the doors.

"Why? What's going on? Who were those guys?" I asked her but did as she said. I would run if she said to, judging by the way these two acted I knew that I had to listen but I also wanted to know what was going on.

"Really, really bad people." Greta told me as she gripped my hand and we ran down the road back home.

CHAPTER 3

TUTTO E TROPPO meaning, "much and too much". An Italian diner where customers could enjoy homemade Italian food from the comfort of a rebranded and refurnished vintage train that hadn't been running for well over a decade. The owner of the restaurant, a short and fat man by the name of Carlo, was a close "buddy" (his words) of my father's.

They drank together, and gambled together, getting into the occasional fight because one accidently spent all the money that he had on him on their gambling games and lost. My father claims that they have known each other ever since they were teenagers and Carlo was someone that he trusted and viceversa.

I was one of the four waitresses that Carlo had and all of the waitresses were Italian beauties. They had perfectly tanned skin, dark eyes, dark and long hair that bounced and flowed on their backs. With the exception of a single girl's preferred make up look, they almost looked like Italian models who stepped out of an Italian magazine. They were tall and slim, with eyes so intense, they could give Bella Hadid a run for her money.

The uniform that we were required to wear was a red and white checked dress that gave a classic retro look and feel, with a sweet streamer collar with embroidery, wide cuffs and a wide skirt that flared out in a way that gave you the feel of a dancer or those sexy waitresses you would see on TV.

There was a tiny bindable apron that we tied around our waists and we had to wear a white pretty hat with red embroidery, spelling out the name of the restaurant. The dress was short and reached just below the butt and if you weren't careful when you bent over, then the diners would obviously get a peek of your ass. Our uniform included a pair of red platform heels that added an extra seven inches to my height and were not at all comfortable but, there was no way to complain.

"Good, good," Carlo purred as I stepped out from the back to show him how the uniform looked on my figure. I was not supermodel thin like the other waitresses but I was slender, and the uniform fit me well. Carlo stroked his beard as he looked at me from bottom to top before his brown beady eyes met my own and he let out a crooked smile. "you look good. The customers will be happy."

I shifted uncomfortably from foot to foot because this wasn't me. I tugged a bit at the skirt, trying to make it longer but it didn't help. I was highly uncomfortable because this wasn't like me at all, "I think the skirt might be a bit too short." I said softly as I looked back at Carlo who shook his head at me.

"What? Absolutely not. It's perfect." He told me in broken Italian. "now come on, you must get ready to take orders with Elena." He grabbed my wrist and began to pull me behind him while I struggled to keep up with him as he led me to the front of the store where the other waitresses were moving about with ease and grace. "Elena, help Delaney." He said as he let go of my wrist once we approached Elena.

Elena had her long luscious hair in dramatic extra-large waves all gathered by a ribbon on the top of her head. She stood at 5'9 and looked back at me with dark eyes, lined by dark lashes in pure boredom and contempt as if I wasn't worthy of her time. She didn't say anything, just glanced back at Carlo and said something in Italian and Carlo nodded his head and walked to the back.

She looked back at me, "quanto è buono il tuo italiano?" she asked me and I looked at her with confusion. She saw the blank look on my face, "how good is your Italian?" she repeated in English, her tone even more disappointed. She walked around the counter and signalled for me to follow behind her. I saw her grab a notepad off the counter.

"Erm, not that good. I don't know any Italian, in fact." I said nervously as she walked us over to a booth where her and the two diners all began speaking in Italian. Elena effortlessly spoke to the diners who were an elderly couple, a couple who poorly disguised their shock and horror at me standing there. They said something to Elena and she turned to look at me before she looked back at them and smiled, and replied, "sì, è nuova." (yes, she's new).

She turned and signalled for me to follow, "this is an Italian restaurant, in an Italian town. You have to learn Italian because most of the diners don't know English." She told me as she ripped the page off the notepad and stuck it to the window connecting the kitchen to the front counter.

She placed the notepad back onto the counter and looked back at me before she raised her hands towards my direction. "I'm fixing your hair," she told me, looking at me to see if I would protest but I wasn't sure so I just looked at her. She brought her hands to my hair and began to play around with my ginger coloured 12 inch hair that reached by my shoulders. I didn't understand what she was going to do with my hair because it was bone straight with all evidence of my curls gone.

She gave up and leaned against the counter. "let me tell you a bit about this place. We get diners of all ages- teenagers, kids, couples, old people. And they will be a bit, what's the word...uh, maybe... apprehensive, yes that sounds about right," she said with a proud nod to herself, "when they see you but it's because there aren't any, you know," she paused for a bit and gave me a raised brow, "black people in this town. However, there are certain hours of the day that you might notice...uh...the diner clearing out to make space for VIP individuals. When they arrive," her face suddenly turned deathly serious, "you do not make eye contact with any of them. You don't say anything out of turn, whatever they want, they get."

I furrowed my eyebrows, "how will I know who these people are?" I asked her.

"Oh, Delaney," she shook her head as the chef rung the bell to show that the food was ready. "you'll know." she turned and picked up to bags of food that was wrapped and ready to go. "but lucky for you, you're about to meet them." She said and walked away back to the table where the elderly couple was seated.

They got their food and handed a few notes to Elena who smiled at them and they got up and headed out. As I looked around the then busy and rowdy diner, the place was thinning out with all the diners making their way out. All the waitresses quickly cleared out and cleaned the tables, making sure that there was little evidence of other diners having previously been there. I stood behind the counter and watched them before my eyes were drawn to the outside, looking through the window there was a sudden chill that ran up my spine as I saw several blacked out BMW's making their way and parking right outside the diner.

I remembered the deathly afraid look on my sister's face and how tightly she had gripped onto my hand when we had to run home. She kept looking over her shoulder, and once we got home she and her parents gathered in the kitchen together and terrifyingly whispered to each other. When I asked what was going on, Gabriela and my father, Alessandro shrugged it off and laughed as if there was no problem and encouraged me to go to bed to be fresh and ready for work.

Even though I so desperately needed to know, I let it go. Yet here were the very people that had frightened Greta and the gas station boy, Lorenzo. Elena walked back towards me. Her eyes were hard and strict, "don't make eye contact. You never look any of those men in the eye." She said between gritted teeth before she pulled me discretely behind the counter.

I looked down at the register, attempting to not look up but I couldn't help my curiosity when Elena made her way to the front with the two other waitresses on her tail. I looked up at the door to see men in black suits entering the place, quickly filled out the cabin. They were loud and rambunctious, laughing and chatting away in Italian. I watched them each walk through the entrance until a certain individual who wasn't wearing a black suit entered the diner.

The man was wearing a stone blue three piece suit and his presence in itself let me know that he was in charge. He was tall, 6'8 tall and he had the most rich long black curls that I have seen on a man. His hair was as dark as night and he had a neat stubble decorating his face. I knew that I was supposed to look away, but hell, I couldn't. The music in the background was playing Back to Black by Amy Winehouse and it was during the part of the chorus when this strange man's eyes roamed the room and in milliseconds collided head on with mine.

Amy's smooth voice played, echoing on the inside of my head as hardened grey eyes looked into my own, stripping me naked of thoughts and reasonable actions. I couldn't breathe, only blinked once in a million years as everything else seemed to fall away.

He was by far the most handsome man that I have ever seen in my life and I was taken aback.

I don't know when common sense returned but it was too late. However, I managed to finally avert my eyes as I remembered Elena's warning words and looked away, looking down at the register but still feeling the burning gaze of the curly haired giant that had strode through those doors. I fiddled around with whatever I could put my hands on, my hands terribly shaking from how intense that moment had felt.

"Delaney," I looked up at the mention of my name and saw Elena standing in front of me with an uneasy expression.

"Yeah?" I answered, wondering if she saw the way that I ogled the man.

She held out her notepad and pen towards me, "he wants you to take his order."

I raised an eyebrow, "what?" I stammered, trying to think of what to say. "but I don't know any Italian."

"He doesn't care. Go." She told me with a look that said that I had no choice and to stop wasting time.

I nervously swallowed and looked around the diner noticing that it was suddenly silent, so silent, that if I were to drop a pin it would sound like an explosion. I looked back at Elena and nodded my head, taking the notepad from her and walking around the counter. I didn't know where to put my eyes, because wherever I looked, I felt the heavy stares of the tens of men filling the diner. I had to walk all the way to the back of the train, to where the curly haired man sat.

When I reached his booth, he was seated all alone.

This time, however, I didn't look at him. I looked down at the notepad and begged my hands to not tremble. "hello, my name is Delaney and I will be your server. What would you like to order?" those were the words that I found most fitting to say at this moment. Elena hadn't even given me the specific run down on what I had to say to diners, so I put all knowledge that I had gathered from watching American movies all my life, to use. I thought it would be courteous to introduce myself and simply ask for their order, right?

There was silence in response and I began to doubt if he had even heard me. I looked up from the notepad to meet those hardened grey eyes that observed me. My unsuspecting brown eyes collided with his just as they did moments before. Suddenly, I forgot what it was that I had to do and I stood there in the presence of a man whose aura was choking me, causing goosebumps to appear on my arms.

He leaned back in his seat, tilting his head and placing a hand covered in tattoos and rings on the table. There was an unexplainable look that crossed his face, "what's a woman as breath-taking as you…" he paused, drumming his fingers on the table, "doing in a town like this?" he asked me. His voice was like sultry heaven. It wasn't deep and angry, but sultry and seductive, as if he could talk a snake out of its own skin. It had a certain stern to it that let me know that he was in charge.

Hearing what he said made me feel bashful, and I broke eye contact and looked down at the notepad, trying to hide the bashful expression on my face. "I should really just take your order." I decided to say as I held the pen just an inch off the notepad.

"My usual." He responded and I nodded, deciding to keep any doubts to myself and would just tell Elena that he wanted his usual and she would probably know what that was.

"Coming right up." I said with a smile as I turned on my heels and walked away. As I returned back to the counter, the place was still drop dead silent and only then did I realise, that everyone had heard every word that had been said.

Chapter 4

The rest of the week proved to be anti climatic because the tall man in the stone blue suit and his entire "crew" had gone MIA. However, I would like to say that the rest of the town seemed to be happy about this, and while I pretended to understand why they felt this way, I was in fact curious about the tall man and wondered where he could have disappeared to. I know it's not my place and I definitely should not be wondering about the kind of man who causes people's faces to flash with deathly fear and terror as if the mere mention of him would result in total execution.

Following the events that transpired on my first day, Carlo had appeared from the back and pulled me into a bone crushing hug with my arms by my side as he heartly laughed and told me that I was a "good employee, very, very good waitress!" in his crooked English as though proud of the attention that I had gotten from the curly haired man.

"Hey, Elena, can I sit next to you?" I asked timidly as I entered the staff cabin where she was sitting and enjoying a simple sandwich. She had been looking outside the window, taking in the view of the bushes surrounding the back of the train, the side of the train that Carlo hadn't cared to take care of as much as he took care of the outside of the train that was visible to diners.

Her eyes found mine and she slowly nodded, grabbing the bottle of water that she had placed beside her sandwich and drinking from it. I slid into the booth and I pulled out my own lunch that Alessandro had put together for me. He had insisted on packing my lunch for me. I opened the pink and white lunch bag, and I peered at the contents inside. Alessandro had neatly packed a juice box for me, along with an apple and a yellow packet of salted Lay's. At the bottom of the lunch bag was the large clear rectangular lunch box that held the two slices of bread perfectly cut into four with a little butter smeared inside for me to place the Lay's crisp and have a crunchy lunch.

For a moment, I hesitated in taking out the lunch and just looked at how beautiful and neatly packed the food was. I remembered watching Alessandro recite to me what was in lunch bag as he carefully zipped it up and looked at me with wide and nervous eyes. The back of my throat began to burn and a lump formed in my throat as I thought about how something as simple as Alessandro making my lunch for me, made me feel special.

My mother used to do the same thing. And I was forced every morning to watch Gabriela lovingly prepare school lunch for her children, watching as she bent down and kissed them each on the cheek and forehead while I would just sit around the island and stuff a spoonful of cereal in my mouth to stop myself from crying. However, Alessandro had been packing my lunch for me ever since I started working, and he even went as far as dropping me off right at the door of the diner and even though I would just sit there and give him an awkward smile or some shrug and a bland "goodbye", I would enter the diner and rush to the bathroom before locking myself in a stall and silently crying.

"Are you okay?" Elena's voice broke me out of whatever spell that I was under and I paused, registering her words. Her tone sounded confused and partially concerned. I suddenly cleared my throat, and quickly pulled the items out of my lunch bag.

"Yeah," I said as I cleared my throat again and didn't bother looking up at her because I knew that my eyes were still glossy and would give me away.

She let out a light laugh, "your lunch bag," she pointed towards it, "it looks like it's for a kid." She laughed again, not mockingly though, or maybe she was but I just didn't pick it up.

I tried to laugh with her but it came out forced. "yeah," I paused as I pulled it off the table and placed it on my seat, "I guess it is." I didn't mind it being so childish, but I wouldn't tell her that.

Elena fell silent, "hey," she called for my attention and I looked up at her with questioning eyes. She furrowed her eyebrows, her features turning serious and concerned, "are you sure you are okay? You look like you want to cry."

I let out a wide smile, "yes, I'm fine," I said with a dismissive wave as I tore open my packet of crisp and laid out the Lay's along the bread. "so Elena, there's something that I want to ask and I can't think of asking anyone better than you." I was adjusting well to my job and I had even picked up some Italian. Having been spending so much time around Italians, who spoke

Italian, it was a bit easier to pick up on the language but I was definitely no expert.

The girls in the diner weren't too much of a problem, they didn't go out of their way to talk to me and definitely treated me like an outsider while the only person who would actually talk to me was Elena. However, if you were to meet the other girls you would think that Elena was a total bitch because of her resting bitch face, but she has been as much of a sweetheart as Elena could be. I didn't go out much, so I considered Elena to be a friend even though I don't think that she would say the same.

She finished her sandwich and shrugged, folding her arms and then placing her elbows on the table as she looked at me. "okay."

"How long have you been living here?" I asked her, beginning to eat my lunch as she tilted her head and easily responded to my question.

"I was born and raised here, however my parents are immigrants from Rome, Italy. Why?" she asked me.

I looked over my shoulder, making sure that there was nobody else around, "I mean," I looked back at her and kind of lowered my tone, "I, kind of, want to know who the dudes are with the blacked out BMW's." I gauged her face, looking for a reaction.

She was silent, and just as I did before, she looked over her shoulder and looked around to make sure that it was just the two of us. "they are really bad people, Delaney." She said, her voice just above a whisper and her words careful.

"I've heard that, but the question is how? How are they bad people? What did they do?"

She leaned in, "in this town, we don't ask around about these people, Delaney. You could get us killed." She paused and shook her head as if she couldn't believe what she was doing, "those people are a part of the Italian mafia. The Italian mafia is huge, it's a huge crime family and they have this thing of expanding their wealth and power by going to different places and having a certain member of that family run business there. Are you understanding what I'm saying?" she didn't wait for me to respond but there was no need because my neck moved with speed. "they are dangerous, the kind of dangerous where if you get mixed in with them and their 'business' matters your body is chopped into pieces and mailed to your family as a message."

I gasped and looked at her with wide eyes, not believing her words. Mafia? Lord, I thought that was just something that happened in the furthest corners of the globe. I wasn't stupid, I knew the mafia existed. I'm from South Africa, and gangs and gang wars were far too common. Of course, the French Mafia, Mexican cartel and Italian mafia were far too famous to be surprised by this information. I was just shocked that I was in a place with those kind of people. "and that, that guy who wanted me to be his waiter?"

She lowered her voice even further and leaned in and I did the same. "he's the leader, the Caporegime, and he is very..." she put her fingers to her head, rotating them in a motion that explained crazy. "he's a cold blooded killer and his cousins with the Italian mafia don in Italy. There are horror stories about him, but around these parts, we call him "dono della morte"."

I furrowed my eyebrows, "what does that mean?" I asked her, eager to know more.

"His torture methods are so gruesome that, from him, death seems to be a gift. Dono della morte means "gift of death". His real name...is a mystery to everyone who's not in the mafia."

CHAPTER 5

Sleep rarely came easy to me nowadays, and even when it did, I couldn't asleep for more than two or three hours. I tried everything. I tried falling asleep later than everyone else who would have their bedtime at 9 o'clock. So Alessandro would leave me with the TV remote and leave me to enjoy whatever late night television shows would come on. So I would usually end up asleep on the couch sometime past midnight and at around three or so, I would wake up and just lay there with my eyes wide open, looking at the TV screen that I had forgotten to turn off, play whatever programme was running at that moment.

This night was different because I fell asleep earlier. At 8 o'clock, I could barely keep my head on my shoulders so I went to bed, my feet aching from the painful shoes that I had to wear at work. I woke up sometime after 1 o'clock, and when I looked next to me, Greta's feet were practically in my mouth. She was a terrible sleeper, always kicking and fighting in her sleep. The gag is, she's sleeping on the floor tonight, but somehow managed to get her feet on the bed and begin kicking me. Her arms were sprawled out and her hair was put into a neat bonnet. Her mouth was wide open and she was snoring loudly.

I was usually the one who slept on the floor, but I didn't mind that. Alessandro felt bad about it and promised to buy me a bed as soon as he gets his next pay check but I don't want him to, because there's barely any space left in the bedroom. I assumed Greta didn't want to wake me up and just opted for the floor.

I couldn't bring myself to just lay there and look up at the ceiling, so I just stood up and climbed off the twin bed. I went over to Greta and carried her onto the bed. She was mighty heavy and she was a heavy sleeper so she didn't even budge as I dragged her to her bed. I let out a heavy breath as I finally set her body on the mattress before I grabbed the blanket and threw it over her.

I looked around the dark room before I thought to head to the kitchen and maybe sit there instead.

I was uneasy and uncomfortable all of a sudden.

I walked out of the bedroom and made my way to the kitchen, trying to be as silent as I could. I poured myself a glass of water but could barely swallow a single drop of it because I suddenly felt homesick. I missed home- my real home. I missed the way that my own bed felt and the bounciness of the mattress. I missed the way my home looked, the way that the doors of my wardrobe were being kept up by elastic bands and duct tape. I missed the way that my home smelled of Sta-Soft (fabric softener) and pine gel (surface cleaner). Hell, I missed the way that my water tasted.

And soon enough, sitting on that couch and staring at the TV blankly didn't help me one bit so I just stood to my feet and made my way out the door. I didn't even care to put on a pair of shoes, all I did was chuck my bonnet off my head and leave it on the couch. I, as silently as possible, turned the key and managed to open the door without so much as a squeak. I know that it's not the bravest or wisest decision but I just needed to take a breather. I needed some air. I felt suffocated.

I closed the door behind me and promised myself that it was only going to be a five minute walk up and down the street and I would come back as soon as possible and no one would notice that I was ever gone.

I closed my eyes and smiled, embracing the chilly air that hit my exposed arms. I was barely dressed, only wearing a white tank top with one of Alessandro's basketball shorts that I wore to bed. I was barefoot and I regretted not having worn my glasses because I could barely see but I didn't care. It felt good to get out of that house and just be alone, with no one else surrounding me. I enjoyed the feel of the ground beneath my feet and I began to hum to La Vita Nuova, remembering how I had fallen in love with opera because of this masterpiece song and a very special music teacher who saw the world in me.

I had been so lost in my own mind and so accepting of this peaceful time that I failed to notice the approaching figure on the road that was no where near Alessandro's house since I hadn't been paying attention. I only noticed too late when a pair of the world's shiniest and most expensive looking shoes aligned with the steps of my bare feet and I heard a voice that I just couldn't get out of my mind, "are late night walks common for young women where you're from?" the words were sultry and almost teasing.

I gasped and looked up, looking into grey eyes that haunted me even in my most beautiful of dreams. The grey eyes of the man that I was told was a killer and a leader in the Italian mafia. "huh?" was all that I could say because I was at a loss for words.

"Don't you know that monsters come out to play at night?" he continued, looking ahead while I was so drawn to him and his very existence. He was so much more good looking up close. Goodness, how was it possible for a man to look this...hot?

I struggled to speak, my mind being overrun by thoughts of how devilishly handsome this man was. "I needed some air," I finally managed to say, clearing my throat and looking ahead. I didn't bother to ask how he was suddenly walking beside me, or anything sensible that any other human would have possibly asked. I did, however, realise who this man was and if Elena's words were anything to go by, I had to keep my distance. "I should head back..." I paused looking around me to see which home it was, so I faulted in my steps a bit. "I should go...in...that direction," I said as I finally managed to see which street I was walking on.

I was about to leave but I wasn't really going to. I stopped in my steps and looked up at him, "where did you come from?" I asked him, wondering what he was doing at a time like this. He peered down at me, his grey eyes and lips pulled into a dark smile.

"Just visiting a friend, in that house over there." The house he nodded his head at, I only noticed now that it's lights were still on unlike the rest of the neighbourhood where all the homes looked dead. I should have known that he obviously didn't have a friend, especially not here but I was too naïve and silly to think straight. I was also too oblivious, or maybe he was just that good, hiding the blood that covered his knuckles that he held in a fist behind his back.

"Oh."

He didn't break eye contact, his eyes still holding mine, "run along now, la mia colomba autunnale (my Autumn dove)."

Hours later- during those very VIP hours of the day where the entire diner is empty except for the VIP's- I sat in a booth across from the curly haired man as I watched the steam from his usual mug of coffee. His "usual" consisted of a cup of coffee and a breakfast sandwich. It was so simple that it was eyebrow raising how he could order the same thing all the time, never changing his order or even requesting for more sugar for his coffee. But then again, I doubt anyone would want to upset him so I'm sure the coffee is made in the exact manner that he prefers.

I was taking his order and he invited me to sit down when I had brought his order for him. It didn't help either that the diner went silent as they did the other day. I knew that this would get me more glares from the other waitresses and possibly even my own death. I was supposed to stay far away from this man but here I was, bumping into him in the dead of night, and now sitting across him in his booth.

He slowly stirred his coffee, his grey eyes on me. They were as hard as steel, and they looked as deadly as the angry ocean. He gave no emotions away, his face was blank and he simply stared at me. I don't know how long he's been stirring his coffee but finally he placed the tiny teaspoon on a napkin that he had neatly folded for himself. "I can't get you out of my head," he said with a smirk as he looked me up and down, his eyes taking their time to take me in.

I blushed, looking down and breaking eye contact as I nervously fidgeted with my hands that were rested on my lap. What was I supposed to say to that? He paused, the cup almost to his lips, his gaze so powerful that it felt like he was stroking every inch of my skin that his eyes ran over, "what's your name, Autumn dove?" he let out in a sultry toned low whisper, as if he knew the way that my body would respond with goosebumps and butterflies in my stomach.

I didn't want to talk to him, because I was suddenly self-conscious about my raspy toned voice. I worried about something as silly as not sounding as good as he does. I bit my bottom lip, my eyes still not looking into his, "Delaney Dardan," I responded lowly.

He hummed in response, placing the cup back on its saucer before he spoke up, "that's not your father's last name." I didn't care to wonder how he knew about my father because I figured that I was the talk of the town as it was and everyone knew that the new black girl in Merton was Alessandro's daughter. "how are you liking Merton so far?" he asked me and I let out a nervous smile, tucking my hair behind my ear in a way that was not like me at all.

I was not the kind of girl who tucked her hair behind her ear, yet here I was- my mother was probably rolling in her grave. "it's nice." Was all that I could awkwardly say, hyper aware that the diner was drop dead silent and everyone could hear every word said and this was not at all private.

"Just nice?" he let out a low chuckle, shaking his head, "I can't have that." He picked up his cup, taking a long sip of the hot coffee, "how about..." he paused, running his hand through his hair and leaning back into his seat. "I show you all there is to Merton, while we wine and dine?" my eyes slowly trailed their way back to his orbs and I felt my heart skip a beat.

I swallowed, thinking about what he just said. I opened my mouth to answer, thinking about letting him down easy but somehow my eyes made their way to meet with Elena's dark eyes. She stood so far away, that I wondered how in the hell her gaze compelled me. She mouthed the words "yes" with wide eyes and my eyes went back to the grey eyed man, "yes."

I had a feeling that the reason that she wanted me to say yes was because you never told him "no".

Chapter 6

I was in no way, shape or form, the kind of girl where things revolved around her. I rarely had "main character" moments and I was always the side character who got to say one line every four or five episodes. I didn't mind it though. I didn't like attention being on me or being in the limelight. The life of the shadows was enough for me. Even at school, I wasn't popular. I sat with the nerdy kids and we had our own inside jokes about certain popular students. I preferred to rush home immediately after school, and spent all of my free time watching TV or being on social media, liking funny videos and pretty pictures instead of being the girl in the pictures.

My mother was always the centre of attention, always the one that everyone's energy gravitated towards. She could walk into a dental office and make every one laugh and become friends with whoever was there, she was the kind of woman whose smile literally lit up a room because she had the most beautiful pearly whites and her grin was contagious. She could never just smile, she always grinned from ear to ear, displaying rows of perfect white teeth with a gap in between her two front teeth.

Her African woman features sat in such a perfect way on her face that it was so painfully obvious why men would fall at her feet.

I sat at Gabriela's dressing table, peering into my own eyes and tearing apart my reflection, trying to find traces of my mother. My mother's lips were full and wide, while my lips were bottom-heavy. She had a broad nose, while mine was small. Her eyes were wide and doe-like while mine were upturned. Her cheeks had been full and that seems to be the only thing of hers that I have.

She had a chestnut complexion while my skin was a honey tone. The end of my cheeks had a light blush to them, and my mother and grandmother loved to tease me about it. But the most beautiful of all, was the litter of dark freckles that covered my nose and spread across the top of my cheeks. I have been insecure about them my whole life because when I was in Primary school, kids would tease me and say that I had spots of dirt on me. I have come to love them, but some days, I do cover them up with makeup.

I placed my hands around my face, delicately cradling my face as I imagined it to be my mother. There were so many moments when my mother would just cradle my face in her hands and her eyes would glance over every inch. Her warm brown eyes seemed to be filled with so much wisdom and carefree nonchalance that adults rarely had. That's another thing I got from her; her eyes. My eyes were a warm brown and when I stood in the light they almost looked hazel even though they weren't.

I had makeup on, of course I did- I had a date with the kind of man that you're supposed to stay away from. Carlo let me go home earlier than usual, which is a big deal because he loves to work us to the bone, until there's not a dollar more that he can make from diners. When I arrived home, I should have been suspicious to find the house empty since Gabriela doesn't work and is always home. But that was the last thing on my mind because when I arrived home, there was a brown box with a red bow placed on the counter with a letter from the man himself.

Inside the box was a dress, a fur coat, and another smaller box inside that contained all the makeup products that I could use. There was no other place to get ready other than Gabriela's dressing room and I hoped that she wouldn't mind. I made sure to clean up any mess that I had made.

I knew how to apply makeup. That was one of the many things that I had picked up from YouTube and the years of watching YouTube makeup artists. I would experiment with my mother's makeup and by the age of 17, I was so good I could have went pro but my grandmother didn't think that was a real job and told me to forget about it. Applying makeup felt therapeutic to me; the routine, and the end result and creating magic with your face. It just soothed me and put me at such peace because I always did my makeup in silence, never saying a word and making sure that nobody else was around.

The makeup products were expensive and did their job far better than the fake makeup products my mother would buy from China City for me to use. I picked up the red lipstick, it being the only lipstick available for me from the products that 'dono della morte' provided. Dono della morte...understanding the meaning behind it, reminded me how dangerous this was.

I sighed, applying the red lipstick across my lips, watching them turn into a satisfying and pleasing red lip, that went well with my blush and highlight. My hands found my hair which I had put into a low bun, letting a few strands of hair frame my face in a way that made me appear young and not so serious. I stood from the dressing table and walked over to the bed, putting on the pair of Giuseppe Zanotti ankle strap snake heels that caused goosebumps to appear all over my arms. I stood up straight and my eyes immediately went to the full length mirror that was in Gabriela's dressing room, catching my reflection.

I was wearing a birdy grey satin mini dress that reached mid-thigh and when I sat down, rode up past my thighs. The dress had thin straps and had a cowl front that dipped down and revealed the top and inner sides of my breasts in a way that was both tasteful and promiscuous. It was chilly out so I completed the look with a white fur coat.

I seemed to be ready just on time because moments later I heard the doorbell ring and I knew that it was for me. I approached the door, putting one foot in front of the other as I finally rested my hand on the door handle. I let out a nervous breath and when I opened the door I was met with one of the men in black suits. His build towered over mine and I looked up at him, in surprise and shock as to how someone could be so tall. He wordlessly extended his hand with his palm upwards.

I placed my hand in his as he led me to the blacked out Rolls-Royce Phantom that was parked at the end of Alessandro's driveway. The back door of the car was being held open by a man who wore a black and white suit with white gloves. He tipped his hat as I approached the car.

There was clearly no space or time to say anything so I simply and elegantly climbed inside the empty Phantom. The other side of the door opened and the man who had escorted me to the car climbed inside, and had pulled out a fine looking golden glass of champagne that he began to pour a bottle of Ace of Spades in. "thank you," I managed to croak out, unable to believe that I was sitting inside of a Rolls-Royce Phantom, drinking Ace of Spades and dressed in the most expensive outfit of my life.

Was this what it felt like to be the main character? If so, it was dangerously exhilarating. I looked around the expensive interior of the car that I only thought I would ever see online. The starlight headliner that gave the impression of a glittering, starry night sky. I could hear smooth and soft jazz playing in the background and I had to pinch myself to convince myself that this wasn't a dream.

I looked outside when I felt the car come to a slow pace and when I looked, I saw us approaching a large modern mansion that sat on the top of a mountain, overlooking all of the homes. My eyes widened, catching sight of the large gates at the bottom of the mountain surrounded by various men in suits who stood as still as statues. The large black gates were opened for us and the car began to make its way up the mountain, towards the monster sized home that looked like it cost more than just a pretty little penny.

When the car came to a stop outside the steps that led into the home, the chauffeur stepped out of the car and opened my door for me. He tipped his head yet again for me as I stepped out and the man who had been seated beside me in the car had long stepped out and held his hand out for me to place my hand into.

I accepted his hand and let him help me out. I still held the glass of champagne in my other hand and the fur coat had slipped off my shoulders, exposing the strap of the dress and the lowered back for all to see. However, I didn't mind it because however way the placement of the coat, I knew this look was a serve and couldn't be ruined, not with a simple slip of the white fur coat.

The man led me up the stairs and when we walked up the stairs and reached the large glass doors with black metal framing, the doors automatically opened and I awed at the grand size of the foyer that was fit for a fairy tale. "wow." I gasped, taking in the sight of the chandeliers, the high ceilings, the Italian tiles on the floor and the family portraits along the walls.

The curly haired man appeared almost out of nowhere, and I only realised his presence when I heard his voice speak lowly into my ear, "I could say the same." He paused, walking around me before he easily slipped my hand out of the "escort's" hand and placed it in his own. His grey eyes held my own in a powerful and intense gaze before he brought my hand up to his lips and kissed my knuckles, individually. "you look like what dreams are mad of," he stepped closer, his eyes never breaking free from anything to do with me, "magic." He said lowly before he brought his other hand up to brush against my cheek and when he did, all I could do was stare up at him, unable to break free from his grey eyes.

He didn't lie, technically from where we dined, there was not a street or inch of Merton that you weren't able to see. The dinner that the curly haired man had prepared for us was a table for two with expensive wine and fancy cuisine. We sat on the glass covering that covered the pool beneath our feet where stingray swam below. When we had stepped out here, my heart had banged against my chest fiercely, but now that some time had gone by, the fear of the glass suddenly breaking beneath our weight and accidently falling into the never ending abyss of water that was a home for the stingrays- had subsided.

The curly haired man had yet to take his eyes off me. He drunk in my appearance as though I was a rare sight to behold and any moment, I would simply vanish. It made me nervous and put me under pressure because what did I have that drew him in so much? "you know, I've already told you so much about me," I paused as I brought the glass of white wine to my lips, my innocent brown eyes meeting his own grey ones that looked like melted iron. He was leaned back in his chair, his food only partially touched and his glass of white wine empty. His eyes practically devoured me and it made me feel...exposed. "but I don't even know your name."

I had enjoyed every bite of the seven course meals prepared by his chef, and I left nothing on my plate. But in my defence, it was all small portions, that even a toddler would complain of hunger. However, since I was nervous, I didn't have much of an appetite so I was satisfied with the small portions. I watched as he ran his tongue over his bottom lip, his lips stretching into a smirk. "there's a certain way in which the moon just reflects off your skin..." he tilted his head, his voice lowering into a suggestive tone that caused my nipples to harden, "I wonder...how you would look completely bare and naked, underneath the stars," his smirk slowly fell as if what he was saying, he didn't want me to take as a joke, "underneath me."

My cheeks felt hot and I averted my eyes because never had a man spoken to me like this. This was foreign and it didn't help that it was coming from a man who resembled a fallen angel. "I...I'm not that kind of... girl." I stammered, clearing my throat and downing the rest of the white wine, hoping the alcohol would wash over my nerves and get me to not blush at every word that he said.

"You don't have to be any sort of person to have a little fun, or to even," he paused, sitting upright, his voice calling for my gaze to meet his own but I denied the call out of shyness, "abide or explore your desires, my Autumn dove." I had noticed that he called me by that nickname and when I had asked why it was Autumn dove, he stated that it was because of my 'strawberry blonde' hair, to which I corrected him and said that my hair was ginger but I had a feeling he was set on strawberry blonde and there was nothing that could change his mind.

My lower belly fluttered at his words, and suddenly the wine seemed to make my blood warm, making me soft and reactive to his words that washed over me like silk. The cold air nipped at my skin and my nipples were so hard that I knew he could see the hardened buds through the satin material of the expensive dress that he had bought for me. I heard his chair move across the floor and I looked up, suddenly meeting his gaze.

I peered up at him, unable to break eye contact and unable to say a word. There was an intensity behind those eyes, an intensity that I couldn't define but would foolishly believe to be desire. His eyes were captivating and enchanting, bidding me to listen and forcing my body to obey his words and let him have his way with me. "I'm a good girl," I suddenly found myself whispering when he easily stalked before me until he was bent over in front of my face. His face inches from my own and his breath fanning my face in a way that I could smell the whisky on his breath and the scent of Cuban cigar. His eyes almost sparkled at what I said.

"I know," he said in a tone that sounded pleased to hear that. "that's why all I could think about throughout dinner," his fingers found their way to the straps of my dress and easily slid them off my shoulders, "was burying my face between your thighs and feasting on that sweet, little cave of yours." His words were like a shock wave, causing every inch of my body to quiver uncontrollably. He didn't once break eye contact, his eyes held mine making sure that I heard every word that he said, making sure that I understood exactly what he was about to do.

I had a feeling that I didn't have a choice, and this was all about to happen whether I wanted it to or not. However, the way that my body reacted, I had a feeling that it would happen because I wanted it to.

His fingers danced along the skin of my arms, before making their way to my boobs where his thumbs lightly caressed my virgin untouched nubs, and I sucked in a breath. "I want to suck on the sweet nectar that comes from your cunt," he said as he brought his lips closer to mine, that if I were to so much as gasp, they would touch. My lips parted in shock, unable to say a word at the sudden change in behaviour both from him and from my own body. Even though we were outside, and it was chilly, my body was on fire.

His hands made their way to my thighs and gripped onto the flesh in a strong grip and I could feel the dress slipping off my upper body, exposing my boobs to the night air and basically the whole of Merton. I should be stopping him, telling him that I'm not the kind of girl who just allowed any man to touch or even refer to my most lady of parts in vulgar slang. Instead, I just gazed into his eyes, unable to break away from the trance. "let me." he said as he ran his tongue along my lower lip. I felt his hands massage the flesh of my thighs. "open your legs," he ordered in a sultry voice as though that was the only thing I had to do, as though it was the only choice that I had. "open up and let me eat that pussy."

I couldn't stop myself, I had to do what he said. I found myself opening my legs at his command and he whispered against my lips, "good girl," he said proudly and I felt the butterflies set flight in my stomach as I watched him lower himself onto his knees. He pushed up the material of the dress, exposing the thong that I had worn tonight, the very one that had been neatly packed in the box that came with whatever I had to wear tonight.

His thumb went to work the sensitive bud hidden between my lower lips, and I threw my head back and gripped onto the sides of the chair that I was sitting on. I instinctively closed my eyes and bit my bottom lip at the sudden and foreign feelings of pleasure. "look at me," I heard him say as he pinched my clit and forced me to keep my eyes on his even though it was the most difficult thing that I had to do since all I wanted to do was keep my head back and process this very moment.

My eyes stayed on his as he placed my left leg over his shoulder, gaining better access to the one place nobody has ever gone, not even my own fingers. "Agostino," he told me, his breath fanning my vagina and I moaned, nodding my head at the revelation of his name, "you'll be screaming it." I couldn't break away from his grey eyes, not even as he licked the slither of my essence that escaped me. His grey eyes didn't let me look away, not when his lips passionately kissed my nether lips, not when his tongue thrusted into and out of my swollen and sensitive pussy- as he likes to say- and I especially couldn't break away from his eyes when he slurped on every bit of my release after what felt like hours of intense pleasure.

CHAPTER 7

I should have known better.

It had all started out so well, the date, the conversation and even when he pushed past one of my boundaries, I couldn't say no. Maybe it was the wine doing the talking, but I enjoyed what he had been doing...at the beginning. Until he brought me back to his bedroom and that's when things escalated, without my consent.

"Please," I pleaded in a strained voice as my body lay beneath his, no longer enjoying the painfully pleasure filled demonstrations that he was doing on my body now that his member was lined at my virgin entrance.

I wasn't ready. I wanted to wait until marriage, or at least until I met the right guy. I hadn't decided yet. My virginity was important to me, because I knew that the person that I chose to share my "innocence" with should be someone who is as pure as me. "It's important to share your energy with someone who won't drain it. You don't want your soul being attached to the wrong kind of guy." My mother would always say and I guess it was very rich of her considering the promiscuous life she always lived. However, she always told me to be better than her, that I shouldn't just let any Tom, Dick and Harry in between my legs, that I had to be careful because boys nowadays are no good, and have never been good.

Instead of listening to my plea, Agostino placed a delicate kiss on my collarbone, his hands that gripped my wrists and held me down made sure that I couldn't fight as he buried his member in between my virgin walls and I could feel them stretch. I cried out, trying to fight against him and his intrusive size that made me feel full, and even though he had made sure that he played with every bit of my body to make me wet it still hurt because I was fighting him. "loosen up for me, Autumn dove," he recited in my ear in that sultry voice that I had loved so much but had never loathed as much as I did in that moment. "let me in," he continued, his hips moving against my own as my legs shook uncontrollably.

The discomfort and pain had been there in the beginning but after a few thrusts and him letting me accommodate his size, the pleasure took over and my body betrayed me. That didn't help me feel any less violated.

I should have known better. I couldn't help but blame myself. What did I expect? Allowing myself to go on a date with a man that the entire town called "dono della morte". Was I so foolish that I thought that we would talk about teddy bears and our favourite cartoon shows? Of course he would expect something in return. Of course he would expect me to give myself to him. And what would there be a need for him to ask? He always took what he wanted.

I dreadfully opened my eyes before I slowly took in his bedroom, checking beside me on the large custom bed that he wasn't asleep next to me. I was the only one in the bedroom and I looked to the opposite side of the bedroom, looking out the wall of windows at the sun that shined perfectly in the room and provided the kind of warmth that you would expect in a beautiful and expensive home.

I couldn't enjoy anything though; my body hurt. I couldn't help but grip onto the expensive black sheets in tight fists and shut my eyes tight, crying and letting out all of my fear. I swallowed when I realised that crying wouldn't help me and I should just leave with whatever that I own. However, the tears didn't stop.

I sat upright, looking around with frightened eyes and gripping the sheets to my chest. My hands began to shake and my heart pounded, worried that he would walk back in any second. I looked around the bedroom, feeling like I was seeing it for the first time. It was so dark and empty, almost everything in the bedroom was black yet the furniture was minimal even though the bedroom was three times the size of Alessandro's three bedroom home. I slowly took the covers off me and looked between my legs, finding myself clean. I remembered him wiping me clean with a warm towel last night, however I had disassociated at that point and had only laid there, staring up at the ceiling.

I tried to search for my clothes but couldn't find them on the floor. I struggled to stand on my feet, my legs wobbly because of the pain that my vagina was in. But I still stood and wobbled, partially limped around. When I couldn't find any article of clothing around me, I just ripped the sheet off his bed and wrapped it around me, not caring that I had no clothes and just desperate to get out of here. I whirled my head around, looking for a way to get out of this room since I didn't know this place. I was scared and I was afraid of what he would do if he would find me here. What if he would call some of his friends to come and have their fun raping the black girl that he so easily fooled?

I suddenly looked and found an elevator, and I realised that it would be much easier to take the elevator instead of wandering around the home. An elevator has buttons and if I press the button that takes me to the lowest level, it could take me to the main floor of the home and I could leave. I walked to the elevator and the doors slid open and when I stepped in and looked at the panel, there were five buttons for five different floors. I pressed the last one, if ever I land on the wrong floor, I can simply press another button until I find the right one. I stood back and watched the doors, waiting to make my way out of here like a bat out of hell.

To think that I had strutted in here with the utmost confidence in the world while his men probably knew that I was going to get violated was shameful.

When the doors opened, they opened on a floor that was completely empty and gave the feel of a dungeon or a basement. I had never been in one before since South African homes rarely had basements, but they were mostly not a thing. The hairs on the back of my arms stood on end the moment I heard several yells. "HELP!" the voice belted out in desperation, fear and panic.

I stood frozen, looking at the place. The walls were made of that one way glass, the kind that was tinted from the outside but transparent from the inside. This, I didn't know until I heard the voices shout again. "please! Help us! Help us!" and that's when I realised that they could see me. My heart pounded and I wondered if I should even venture so far.

I struggled to breathe, my eyes dancing back to the buttons of the elevator, fighting between being a hero or being a coward.

I remembered how helpless I was last night, and if there was someone who heard my sad pleas for rescue, things would have turned out differently. I gripped the sheet around me and sprinted out of the elevator and along the glass walls on both sides of the long and narrow hallway that gave the feeling of walking through a tunnel. I banged on each of the walls, looking for some secret door. "Help! Help us!" the shouts were collective now, several voices screaming bloody murder and my blood ran cold.

I got desperate, wanting- needing to help them. My heart pounded hard against my chest that I didn't know what was louder; their shouts or my heart.

I finally banged on one of the walls and it gave way into the room with a secret door that slid open. However, I wasn't ready for the sight that met me because the moment that I stepped in, I froze. The room was brightly lit, and there was not an inch where light didn't shine with the expensive and bright lights on the high ceilings of the room. There was over 30 people in the room, some already dead on the floors, missing limbs with the world's most horror-filled dead faces I have ever seen. Some swung from chains in the ceilings, dangling upside down with blood pooled below their heads and dislocated or broken limbs. There were two men on the floor who had their lower torso's sawed off and were very much alive and looking at me. In the far corner of the room was a large lion that was happily feasting on one of the people. Its yellow eyes looked at me and it stood to its feet.

My feet were buried in blood- there was not an inch on this floor that was not covered in blood.

Their desperate eyes looked into mine, "help!" they all shouted, their voices like a broken record- a haunted broken record.

When my senses finally returned and I had seen all that I needed to see, a gut wrenching and horror filled scream escaped me. The screams tore past my lips and only worsened when I saw one of the men who didn't have a lower torse begin desperately crawling towards me, however the lion got to him and placed its paw on his back. He screamed in horror as the lion began to tear him apart.

I stepped back, wanting to run but accidentally slipping in the blood and falling face first. I screamed even more, rushing to my feet not caring that the sheet had slipped off. All I could feel was the blood on my naked body and all that I could see were the horrors of this basement. I continued to stumble in my panic, my screams not once coming to a halt as I sprinted as fast as my human legs could carry me out of that room. However, as I turned, I ran smack into someone's hard chest and I didn't care to look at them, I just began fighting and screaming.

I kicked as much as my legs would let me and scratched at whatever I could with my nails. I managed to escape their arms and continued to sprint, leaving bloody footprints on the expensive marble floors, but I didn't get far because two more men in suits suddenly caught me. I feared that I would have the same fate as the people that I had just found so there was no way in hell, I was letting them hold me. "help!" I screeched at the top of my lungs as the two men captured me with ease and evaded each of my desperate and panic filled strikes.

I thrashed around, fighting- feeling that I was being dragged. I felt a pair of hands that I fear that I will never forget their touch until the day that I die. The calloused, experienced hands that had betrayed me. Agostino placed his hands on either side of my face, finally bringing me back into focus of my surroundings. However, all that I could see was him. I looked into those grey eyes, remembering the look in them when he made me orgasm with ease, remembering the look in them when he told me how tight his Autumn dove was, "rule number one, basement," he shook his head as though he were talking to a child, "no, no." He finally said after what felt like an eternity of silence.

He stood up straighter and looked at his men, "take her to my room. I'll deal with her later." He said, and I let out another shrill scream as the men began to drag me since I was still putting up a fight.

"No! No!" I cried out, not wanting to go back, "don't take me back there! Please!"

CHAPTER 8

The tears that poured down my cheeks were uncontrollable, and the hiccups escaped me in a way that words failed to aid in my current situation. I couldn't seem to shake this feeling; this feeling of a heightened sense of fear, dread, and regret. Why did I ever think that Agostino was a good person? Well, I never thought that he was a good person because Elena had warned me about him.

Suddenly, the words that she had said, made all the more sense. I now understand why everyone feared him as much as they did. I understand why Greta had ducked and hid like a bat in a cave when Agostino's men had arrived at the gas station. I understand why all restaurants and places closed whenever Agostino and his men were in sight. They feared that what was happening to me and the people in the basement, could happen to them.

I had been sitting alone for hours. Agostino's men had practically tossed my body like a ragdoll into his bedroom. I had jolted from the floor, rushing towards the door for them to only slam it in my face. I had screeched and cried, pounding my fists on the door and begging for help. When I tried to use the elevator, it was locked and the doors wouldn't slide open. After what felt like hours of sobbing on the floor and rushing to each of the windows, trying to find a way of escaping, I solemnly made my way to his bed and crawled onto it. I pulled my knees to my chest and just stared at the door.

I hadn't showered- I didn't care to. I was far too afraid of what would happen to me. I knew that there was only one person who could get me out of this, and it was the very man who had gotten me into this.

As though he knew how deflated I was at this point, I watched as the bedroom door swung open and Agostino stepped into the bedroom. My breath hitched and I tried to bring my knees impossibly closer to my body as a way of protecting myself. The first thing that I did was look at his hands, checking to see if he was holding a gun or a knife that he would use to kill me. They were empty, but a man like Agostino- I figured didn't need some weapon when his hands were lethal. I should know.

Looking at him now, seeing his usual nonchalant and distant demeanour that gave nothing away- the very thing that I had found attractive about him; I know found terrifying. He looked like the kind of man that was unbothered by a lot of things that would bother any sane person. He walked with the confidence and arrogance of a man who held the world in his hand.

I watched as he shut the door behind him and his fingers began to work his tie, untying the neat work around his neck. I wondered if I should just shoot to my feet and make a run for it, grab the pillows that cushioned my back and threw them at his head as a distraction so that I could make a run for it. However, when my frightened eyes met his own hardened and knowing ones, there was the sudden realisation that there wasn't much that I could do that would allow me to make my escape, and that feeling was bone-chilling.

He tossed off the coat that he had been wearing, letting it perfectly land on the chair that was positioned before his bed. "p-p-p..." I stuttered, unable to talk as Agostino approached me, his body only metres from my own. I couldn't get the words out of my mouth, my heart pounded against my chest as he sat on the bed and his eyes looked all over my still naked body covered in the dried blood of his unfortunate victims.

"Shh," he finally said, caressing my damp cheek in a gentle manner as though his hands weren't the same hands that held me down so that I couldn't put up a fight. "there's no need to cry," he said in his sultry toned voice that didn't reveal any sort of emotion that you would expect to come with the words that he said. Instead it sounded as though he was reciting it off a page with zero interest in carrying out the role in the way that it was supposed to be carried out. His thumb swiped at my tears, but they were easily replaced. "there's no need to be scared...just yet." He added as his grey eyes met my own and my bottom lip quivered.

"Are you going to hurt me?" I asked him, my voice frail and frightened, and it quivered in a way that it had the day that I had held my mother's dead body in my arms, asking for her to wake up even when I realised that there was no way that she would breathe again. "p...please don't hurt me," I begged in a broken whisper.

He ran his tongue along his bottom lip, moistening it as he looked into my eyes as I spoke. I hoped that there would be some emotion behind those orbs, something in them- anything, really. But they were empty, empty in a way that I had failed to notice before because I was so blinded by his beauty. "my basement is a very special and important place for me, Autumn dove. It's where I go to unwind and relax. It's where I go to have a little fun. You understand that, don't you?" he asked me and even though it was the most disturbing thing to hear that torturing people was fun for him, I quickly nodded my head, not wanting to upset him. "the only time anyone goes into the basement, is if I want them there," there was a meaning behind those words. He wanted me to catch it, judging by the long pause.

I nervously swallowed before I slowly nodded my head, showing him that I understood. "can...can I go home now?" I croaked out, hoping that this was the end of the conversation and I would be able to go home after this. I wouldn't dare breathe a word of this to anyone. Besides, I was so disturbed by what has happened, I doubt that I'll even stay another 24 hours in Merton. I'm leaving this place as soon as he lets me go, and I'm going to use my pay check that I have been saving up to get my own place, to high tail it out of here.

He knitted his brows together and looked at me, "you're not leaving." He responded as he gently tucked a strand of hair behind my ear. My lips parted at his words and my heart skipped a beat. He seemed to understand the confusion- maybe even expected it. "there is something about you, Colomba autunnale (Autumn dove). Something very beautiful, innocent, special and naïve about you that awakens this...carnal desire within. You're not leaving because I want you, in every sense of the word that defines 'want'."

I began to shake my head, my tears racing down my cheeks. "no, no, please, no..." I pleaded but he responded by cupping my cheek.

"Women like you are rare, my dove, and even far more scarce for men like me. That day when I first saw you, I just knew," he cupped both of my cheeks and I was unable to pull my eyes away from his. "I just knew that I would never let you go."

His words were a death sentence, and we both knew it. Never let me go? I began to cry silently, shutting my eyes and hoping that I would wake up and this would all just be a dream. He didn't seem all too concerned about my tears, matter of fact he ignored my cries as if they were background noise. "now, come on, let's take a shower. It's been a long day, and I need a good long fuck."

Chapter 9

Agostino allowed me to walk around the home. I knew that I couldn't leave, and escaping seemed to be impossible. Trust me; I tried running out the front door, and then the back door, and then the other back door, but each time, I never got as far as a foot outside the door before I would see security standing rigidly by the doors, guarding the home. I spent most of my time sitting in Agostino's room, unable to find the energy to carry out my day or get out of bed. Today was the first time in a week that I decided to leave Agostino's room and not be the sex slave that's always just there for his pleasure.

I sighed as I wrapped my arms around my midsection and stepped into the third kitchen of the home. The kitchen staff moved about with purpose, and when I entered the room, most of them left, leaving behind the chef who held her hands behind her back. The chef did an almost-bow in my direction- much like all the other chefs had done in the previous kitchens. I pursed my lips, smiling awkwardly at the action, "can I get something to drink?" I asked her as I stood at the entrance, taking slow steps into the kitchen.

She nodded her head, "freshly squeezed juice, freshly made lemonade, grape juice, iced coffee, latte? Which drink would be to your taste?" she asked me.

"Erm, lemonade, please," I croaked out, trying to think about what it was that I wanted to drink even though I wasn't really thirsty, I just wanted to have something to do, to prolong me having to go back to Agostino's bedroom. I looked away from her and around the kitchen. It was large, much like a lot of this home, and much like the other kitchens it was an all white with flat panel cabinets and concrete countertops and floors. It was bright and beautiful and it looked straight out of a magazine. There was not a spot of dirt or dust on any surface.

The kitchen had a glass wall, one that allowed you the perfect view of the outside. However, people from the outside couldn't see anything inside the home. Most of the house was like that and it gave the house a nice touch since the outside of Agostino's home was beautiful with lush lawns, that sprawled far and wide, with views of the mountains in the distance and whichever room you were in, you got an HD view of the sunrise and sunset.

My heart suddenly skipped a beat as my eyes took in the kitchen, and I rushed to look at the chef, to make sure that she wasn't watching me and had no clue what I was thinking at the moment. The chef was currently occupied with draining the juice of the two lemons that she had set on the counter, and she wasn't looking at me. I watched as her hands moved with the kind of speed that had me perplexed as to how it was possible. I noticed that the people who worked for Agostino were always quick with their duties, and knowing him and what he was capable of, I understood that it was probably a matter of life and death.

I swallowed nervously, my ears ringing as my eyes went back to spot the fire extinguisher placed at the far end of the kitchen. I couldn't believe my luck. A fire extinguisher next to a glass wall? This was my ticket out of here. I had walked around enough of the rooms of the house to tell that the home was covered in forestry, but that was some distance away. If I could get there, then I'm sure I would be home free. I didn't care too much about how quickly this was happening, just that I needed to act on it now or else I might never get the chance to.

"Uh," I paused and pretended to look in my pockets, "I think, I think I accidently left my bracelet in the other kitchen." I said as I looked at the chef whose hands had not stopped moving but her head looked up and she looked at me with a blank face. "could you get it for me? it's urgent." Her hands stopped with the lemons and she seemed partially confused but she didn't say anything- but she wasn't moving quick enough for me. "he gave it to me. I need it back." I rushed out nervously (only from what I was about to do) but I gathered that she thought that it was because I lost a bracelet that Agostino gave to me. She nodded her head and moved with urgency out of the room.

The moment that her feet had stepped out of the entrance of the kitchen, I ran as fast as my legs could carry me to the end of the kitchen and grabbed the fire extinguisher. I knew that it was going to make a noise but I'd be damned if I had to spend anymore time in here than I had to. I refuse to let this be the remaining days of my life.

I went to the wall, gripping onto the extinguisher with desperate and strong fists, and slammed it against the glass. The glass cracked, so I slammed the fire extinguisher the second time and it gave way. I didn't care to make sure that I had broken enough of the glass to get through safely. As long as I had made a big enough hole to fit through, I was fine. I threw the fire extinguisher and slammed my body through the remainder of the glass. I had so much adrenaline coursing through my veins that I didn't feel the pain of the shards of glass that stabbed at my exposed arms and my bare feet.

As soon as my body went hurling to the outside and my knees buckled beneath me, trying to catch my balance- I went running. I bolted, not looking behind me or beside me, just desperate to get out of there. If Agostino caught me now, then I would probably be joining his friends in the basement. My breath came out heavy and panicked, my heart pounded and my stomach dropped as I ran through the picturesque lawns and front yard of the notorious gang leader, running towards the tree line in the distance.

God, please don't let them catch me.

I wasn't a runner, I have never been. Matter of fact, whenever we would have Sports day and we would all race, I always came out second to last or last. I didn't care for exercise, and running was simply unnecessary for me. However, at this moment, I was Usain Bolt. In seconds I found myself entering the tree lines and when I did, the ground went from smooth to a mountain rocky since the home was built on a mountain. I'm certain that I stepped on several snakes and other disgusting creatures but there was no way that I cared about that as my feet moved with purpose. All you could hear was the sound of my panicked breath that matched with each of my urgent steps as I curved through trees.

I let out a pained grunt as I slipped over a rock and went tumbling down. My body tumbled uncontrollably, and moments later, in the midst of my tumbling, my head slammed onto another rock and my world went black.

I awoke- I don't know when- it could have been hours later, years later, or even seconds later but when I did, the pain in my head was terrible. I let out a whimper of pain as I struggled to gauge my surroundings. My eyesight slowly returned and when it did I found myself on the floor of the mountain. My face in the dirt and a wet substance running down the middle of my forehead which I was certain was blood. I felt something weird begin to crawl up foot, and I wiggled my toes, trying to get it to stop but when my brain finally registered the feel of scaly skin. I let out a squeal and rushed to my feet. I shrieked, shaking off my leg as I stepped away from the snake which happened to be a cobra that now stood to attention and glared into my eyes.

If there was anything that I was deathly afraid of... it was snakes. Looking now at the Cobra that bared its neck at me and did a slow dance of its movements, I had no idea what to do. Should I turn and run? Could you outrun a snake? Should I stare back at it? Wouldn't it view me as a threat?

The snake didn't seem to be in as much of a dilemma as I was, because unlike me, it didn't hesitant to take action and it struck at me with lightening speed, sinking its teeth into the my exposed calf.

I screamed and I turned to try and run, but I was overcome by a great burning sensation in my calf. I couldn't stop screaming as I limped, trying to get away from the snake. I suddenly heard a loud gunshot, and the bullet sped past me and hit the Cobra. I began to cry when I saw one of the security detail, standing in the short distance, looking casual as if he had simply taken his time to get to me. I wanted to turn and run but I was in pain. I started to cry, much like a child would when they got hurt and needed their mother. The man walked up to me and easily scooped me up in his arms, taking me back to the place that I had so pathetically thought that I could escape.

When he took me back to the house, Agostino was nowhere in sight but I didn't care. My body was sweating from the pain, and it seemed like I had spent an entire hour in pouring rain. I was screaming and crying, my body convulsing in pain as Agostino's private medical team got the poison out of me and tried to calm me down in the process. Two hours later, it was like nothing had ever happened. Sure, my calf was still in pain but it was a bit bearable. I thought that they would let me sleep it off, but the nurse woke me up minutes ago and told me that he wanted to see me.

I stood at the very entrance of the kitchen that I had escaped from, finding Agostino seated at the island in those high and expensive chairs. He was drinking a glass of lemonade, a glass I assume was meant for me that the chef had been preparing. The chef was across from him, silently and with struggle, crushing something and turning it into an almost powder before pouring the contents into a bowl. "Lasciaci." (Leave us) I heard him say to the chef who was visibly sweaty and she quickly nodded, scurrying out of the room.

I still stood at the entrance. "I'm sorry," I suddenly said, realising that being alone with Agostino was dangerous. I looked at the glass wall, finding the hole that I had thrown myself through still there. However, the shards of glass were long gone and the floor was clean.

"Finish off what the chef was doing." He only said as he took a gulp of the lemonade. I nervously swallowed but slowly let my feet lead me away from Agostino and replaced the spot of the chef. I looked down, wondering what it had been that she had been crushing with a brick. I found it to be the shards of glass that had been broken from the wall.

I knew that this couldn't be good.

I looked up at Agostino and when those grey eyes stared into mine, I quickly evaded his gaze and grabbed the brick, crushing the shards of glass into smaller pieces and then trying to make them a bit smaller into powder, before pouring them into the ball that was slowly getting filled up. My arms began to cry out in exhaustion and my fingers were bleeding from the cuts, however I didn't dare complain. I kept it all to myself and just did as he asked. What felt like an eternity of silence later, all of the shards of glass had been crushed into a powder that I had placed into the bowl that was now filled about a quarter way which doesn't sound like much, but trust me, it was.

I placed the brick onto the counter and looked down at my hands, afraid to look up at Agostino. "I'm done." I said in a whisper, not sure where this was going.

He didn't say anything, just slid a spoon in my direction, dragging the piece of expensive metal on his expensive counters. I looked at the spoon in confusion, "eat it." My eyes met his and they widened at his words.

"W-what?" I asked, my voice cracking and afraid, shocked and unsure. He didn't repeat himself, just gave me the usual blank stare. "b-but i-i-it's glass?" I said as though I too weren't sure what I was cutting. My heart skipped a beat and my hands began to tremble. "I'll die, it'll kill me."

"You either eat this bowl of glass, or I kill your father and make you eat him." His sentence was chilling. The sultry toned voice was there, he didn't sound any different than when he would casually strike up conversation with me, which was what made me even more terrified that this wasn't a big deal to him.

Tears began to fall from my eyes, "please, Agostino." I pleaded in a whisper, shaking my head at eating the bowl of glass that I admit I hadn't crushed as finely as I could since the task had been exhausting. But even if I had crushed them as fine as anything, it was still glass. It will cut at my insides and lead to internal bleeding. Even though I pleaded for him not to let me do this, I picked up the spoon with trembling fingers because I knew that he would really kill Alessandro and make me eat from his dead body, and I definitely won't be able to do that. I cried, placing the spoon in the bowl and filling up only the tip of the spoon before I raised it to my mouth.

My mouth suddenly felt as dry as the Sahara desert as my eyes watched the slow rise of the spoon to my mouth, my mind yelling at me not to do this. But I was so afraid that if I didn't do this, then the punishment following this, would be far too severe. Maybe this is exactly what I needed; to die. But I didn't want to die...

I let out a cry of pain as I tried to swallow the glass but it cut at every part of me. "please, please, Agostino!" I begged him, my cries turning desperate as I shook my head but he gave away no emotion. He only watched me. I began to sob uncontrollably, fearing for the safety of Alessandro and his family. Glass or a dead body, or maybe he would make me nibble on my father's fingers while he was still alive?

By the time that I was only four spoons in, I was screaming and crying, every bit of spit that escaped me due to my crying was only blood. I was swallowing blood and glass and it was excruciating. I felt Agostino grab me and grab the spoon in my hand, forcing me to eat more of the glass. I kicked and screamed, trying to fight him but he was too strong. "I'm sorry!" I yelled through a bloody mouth that gargled with blood and open wounds. My words were incoherent and I thought that at this point Agostino would have mercy on me, but he didn't. He let go of the spoon and grabbed the bowl, holding my head still as I kept fighting him.

"Open your mouth, la mia colomba autunnale," (my Autumn dove) he instructed as he gripped the sides of my mouth and forced my mouth open before he poured the remainder of the glass into my mouth. Most of it didn't fit in my mouth, and spilled out, but he slammed my jaw shut forcing me to swallow. I scratched at his face, pulling his curly hair and fighting to spit out the contents but he didn't let me, he didn't let me escape until I swallowed the glass and when I did, I felt my body go into overdrive.

He let go of me and at the right time too because my trembling body began to spew blood. I let out a horrified gargled scream as blood escaped me and my insides felt like pure hell. It was just as painful as the snake bite, maybe even worse because the room started to spin and I couldn't focus on anything. My heart raced with a different vigour and my body was in a panic that drove me to a world of darkness as my unconscious face was buried in my own blood.

CHAPTER 10

At first, the sound of distant beeping felt like a tune that played in the far distant parts of my mind. Almost, as though, it was keeping me company in the darkness that I had been surrounded by. It was all that I could hear at times, and other times I heard other voices, and I heard what sounded like a big bang, much like the gun that had gone off in the forest. My body went into more shock, fearful of the meaning behind the bang, even though the memories of that day were still fuzzy- my body knew that something was wrong.

I felt the occasional gentle caress of male, callous hands- hands that could ever touch my lifeless body after months or even years of being dead, my body would somehow shiver. The caress was careful, delicate, and rhythmic, as though he had all the time in the world.

I opened my eyes for what felt like the first time in an eternity, only to shut them when I was blinded by bright lights. I kept those closed for a moment, but I was tired of the darkness and needed to wake up. I needed light. I opened my eyes and when

I did, my head had been turned sideways, giving me the view of an ocean.

I took my time, taking in the view of the brown sand that was outside the glass wall. I watched as a crab walked by, taking its sweet time. Then I looked at the sun that was high in the sky, shining directly into the room and bathing my body in the warmth that only a sun could provide. I watched the way that the sun reflected over the ocean water that was a blue mirror. I looked at the palm trees surrounding the ocean, and I couldn't help the hot tear that escaped my left eye.

It was beautiful. I had never seen something so beautiful.

I would have thought that I had died and made my way to heaven, however, I knew with the continuous strokes on my cheek that I was still living in my hell. I didn't want to look at him, even though I could feel his eyes on me. I took in the view of the ocean, watching the waves form, ride and then crash onto the sand.

I had only ever been to the beach once, and I remember it like it was yesterday. My mother was dating some random man at that point, I never really cared to learn their names because she always seemed to go from relationship to relationship. I don't think she minded though, she loved having her options. I remember the man's name was Prosper and he was a Zimbabwean immigrant who was teaching at a college in Pretoria.

He was married, in fact, he had two wives. A South African wife, and a Zimbabwean wife back in his village in Zimbabwe. It was a random day in December when my mum was running around the home, excited and barely able to keep the grin off her face as she told my grandma to start packing her bags, because

Prosper was going to take us to Durban. My grandma at that point, was tired of giving my mum a stern talking to about the men that she dated, and just shrugged and made her way to the bedroom that she and I shared to pack her bags. After my mum had packed mine and her bags and my grandma was done with hers, Prosper picked us up in his faded silver 2008 Toyota Avanza.

I remember the way that my mum and grandma gripped onto either of my hands tightly as we stood along the edge of the ocean, where the water reached just below my tummy. I wanted to go in further but my mother was paranoid. However, it was the best time in my life. I remember eating the hotdogs that my mum had prepared and stored in her favourite Tupperware and I remember how hard I laughed when my grandma ran from the waves and slipped and fell in front of the thousands of people there.

This beach however, this beach looked like a dream. The water was sparkling clear, you would swear it was fake. The sand was this beautiful brown that looked like burnt glass, and the palm trees were high and rich, with fallen coconuts scattered on the floor.

I tried to open my mouth and speak but it was impossible. The inside of my mouth and throat felt swollen and it didn't help that I had a tube sticking down my throat. That's when I looked away from the ocean and at the grey eyed man who had put me here in the first place. My eyes took in his devilishly handsome features, features that had seemed so breath-taking before I had known what he was capable of. Looking at him now, I asked myself how I could have possibly missed the empty look in his eyes. His curly hair was free and framed his face, it reached just below his earlobes, and the black and rich hair was honestly admirable because how did a man have hair so curly, healthy and beautiful?

"This is one of my other homes," he began, his calm and collected tone immediately reminding me of how he put me in here. "the air is clean and humid, it's quiet and beautiful." He said as he pulled down the blanket that was covering my body and revealed the white gown that I was wearing, that made me look like some 1800's housewife on her way to bed. "I knew that you would love it," he continued as he helped me sit up and I closed my eyes a bit, my body feeling as though I had been hit by a train but I didn't care. It was almost as if he could read my mind. I just wanted to go outside.

He helped me sit up before he pulled my body to the edge of the bed, and I heard the sound of wheels behind me, seeing Agostino pulling some machine behind him. I gripped onto the sheets of the bed, waiting for him to help me up because I knew that my body didn't have the strength. He wrapped his arm around my midsection and helped me to my feet. His arm was strong and sturdy, however, my knees were wobbly, but that didn't seem to be a problem for him but it was for me because I couldn't walk. I took tiny steps. My feet feeling as though I was stepping on pins and needles and it hurt like hell. I gripped onto his skin, my nails digging into his flesh because of how difficult and painful it felt to simply take a few steps.

He walked me to the slider, and we stepped over, placing our feet in the sand. When we did, I let out a happy breath. I enjoyed the feel of the hot sun burning into my eyes, I enjoyed the feel of the humid air on my skin and I enjoyed the feel of the grains of sand in between my barefeet. We walked down the beach, taking tiny steps as we reached the edge of the beach where the waves crashed on land. Agostino sat down on the sand and sat me in between his legs, letting the water of the waves come up our legs with each crash of a wave. I wiggled my toes excitedly, capturing some of the water in my palms and wanting so badly to smile and giggle, run around and dance but the inside of my mouth was beginning to feel as though it were on fire, my lips couldn't move due to the small tube in them and my body felt partially paralysed.

I take that my body was struggling to survive what had happened to it.

Agostino was silent, I felt his hands on my waist, holding me, not in a way that kept me in place but just holding me. I didn't want him to hold me, I wanted him to get his dirty hands off me but there was nothing that I could do. I feared for my life and would let him do whatever that he wanted to do to me.

I felt him begin to brush his fingers through my hair, "you're not the first to try and escape, la mia colomba autunnale, and you will not be the last." He placed a kiss on the side of my neck, just below my ear. My body became rigid, suddenly afraid of being so close to him, and so vulnerable to the water.

Would he hold me down and let the water drown me? A million thoughts ran through my mind. "people could tell you horror stories about me, Autumn dove, and luckily for you, you can chirp in." he pushed my hair to the side, throwing it over my right shoulder as his fingers playing along my exposed neck. "I won't kill you, my Autumn dove, you hear me? I won't. However," he paused, placing another kiss on my spine, running his nose up the curve of bones to the bottom of my hair. "I'll always give you a taste of it, always make you long for it, always make you beg for an escape... just to never give it to you.

This time, it's your voice and your internal organs, next time it will be your limbs, your family, your lineage. I'll take everything from you, my beautiful..." he breathed out, his fingers finding their way in between mine and holding my hands, "beautiful dove. I'll take it all, until I'm the only one left, until I'm all that you have." His words were bone-chilling, and I had yet to let out a breath. I had forgotten to breathe, just listening to what he had to say. "I'll give you this advice once, and once only, don't give me that chance, don't make me do to you what I have done to so many others out there." He turned my face sideways, making me look at him, his eyes taking me in, "you know why?" I shook my head, my eyes wide and afraid as I looked into his grey ones that had yet to give away emotion. "because you're special."

CHAPTER 11

I hated to say it but Agostino knew my body better than I ever did. The quick work of his thumb and index that toyed with my engorged clit, his steady and strong thrusts, his left hand wrapped around my throat, making me struggle to breathe, his occasional dirty words as his face hovered over mine, the curtain his curly hair formed around us, forcing me to look into his eyes-all of it played a role in the way that my back arched, the way that I moaned out his name and the way that the tears slowly rolled down the side of my face as he brought me to yet another orgasm.

It was so good, it was actually becoming a punishment. I cried out, placing my hands on his stomach, trying to stop or get him to slow his harsh pace in and out of me. "please," I begged him, feeling his strong and sturdy chest on my own as I begged for him to stop fucking me because I was on my seventh orgasm and I couldn't take anymore.

He was still as hard as a rock inside me, his cock moving with purpose and pleasure between my tight walls. I clenched around his member. It was thick and long, reaching parts of me that I never thought could be reached, and it only made it feel worse when he placed his hand on my stomach, forcing me to feel all of him. "it's too much, it's too much." I began to chant and cry out as he only seemed to go deeper. I felt his cock throb inside me.

My skin was slick with sweat, and he had me open my legs wide for him. If I were to dare close them, I was subjected to longer durations of his fucking and I couldn't take it. He leaned down and pressed his lips to mine, his lips smacking against mine sloppily in a way that made my already hardened and abused nipples stand. His tongue moved in my mouth, dancing along with my own as he suddenly bit down on bottom lip, but the mix of pain from him biting my lip, his hand around my throat, the other on my clit and his cock relentlessly in my hole- I came yet again, except this time, I took him with me.

My body shook uncontrollably as I laid there, struggling to catch my breath and struggling to get rid of the white all around my vision. I could feel him fill me up with his semen, and the warm liquid made me feel relieved that this was the end...at least for the next few minutes when I could gather myself yet again. Except I was thinking of faking a tummy ache, anything to not have to go through this again because my vagina was swore from the endless hours of sex.

He took his time sliding his cock out of my entrance, all the while his eyes were on mine, making sure that I felt every tiny bit of him. He leaned down and kissed me on the corner of my lips, his fingers now gripping the side of my face in a strong hold, "when I fuck you, you take what I give you. Understand?"

he stated, his grey eyes relaying the message that I was to never beg him to give me a bit of a break.

I didn't respond immediately, my mind was still hazy and I was trying to calm down from the painful high. "yes...sorry..." I said in a hoarse whisper.

It had been a long seven weeks that we were spending in his home on his family's private island that was a few ways away from the islands of Hawaii. I was spending this seven weeks healing from the assault on my body. My throat and most of its pipes had been completely damaged and not to mention the lining around my stomach and some of my vital organs was also damaged. I had underwent extensive surgery when I had slipped into an eight day coma, and when I had woken up, I had to heal. A man like Agostino could afford the kind of medical attention and care that I was getting, I had the most expensive and the best of medicine and specialists who made sure that I was back to the way that I had been before being forced to eat glass.

Now that my body had almost fully, like 98%, recovered, Agostino used this time to make up for all those 7 weeks of no sex and if he wasn't going to take it easy, I was probably going to end up back in that hospital bed from all of his "love-making". I preferred to call it that, even though Agostino was very vocal about his need to "fuck" me. It made me feel a little less used.

I walked on wobbly legs, walking back to his bed after having to relieve myself. He was standing in the corner of the room now, with a pair of sweatpants that hung loosely on his hips, showing off his body muscle. "can... I say something?" I asked him as I sat on the bed, placing my legs beneath my body and sitting, facing his direction. I didn't care that I was still naked, he had already seen all that there was- and he didn't allow me to wear any clothes.

He was pouring himself a glass of scotch whisky while he made me an iced latte. "yes, ask me anything." I knew that wasn't quite true. There were certain things that I was "allowed" to ask, certain things that didn't upset him. These last few weeks have been the most difficult for me, a part of me believes that he was grooming me or training me to only...be for him. To only think of him, see him, know him. I had no contact with the outside world. I spent all of my time with him and I was getting lonely. When I couldn't talk, he seemed to hear all my thoughts and worries, and he would talk here and then- he wasn't talkative but he was definitely speaking out of character for a man like him who would take an eternity to finish a simple conversation simply because he found it silly.

He turned and walked over to the bed. He handed me iced latte and I thanked him. "I miss Alessandro," I finally managed to say, after having sat in the silence that Agostino created. I swallowed nervously, gripping the mug with terrified fingers. I didn't want to upset him. "I just would like to visit them again...it's been long since I have seen him, Greta...and the rest of them. Of course, if you wouldn't mind and it's not a problem and in that case if it is then I'm sor-" I began to ramble.

I felt him gently play with my ear, cupping my cheek at the same time before he made me look at him. "whatever you desire, I will make happen, my Autumn dove. Visiting your family, is important and undemanding. You never have to ask." I nodded my head, looking away from his strong and beckoning gaze.

"In that case..." I paused, biting my bottom lip, the piece of flesh still burning from his biting me. "can I visit my mum and grandma too?"

CHAPTER 12

We definitely looked out of place sitting on the cheap white plastic chairs of Mme Ruby's Takeaways. Agostino's men surrounded the area, making sure that no one dared approach us. The convoy of black Mercedes-Benz that was on the other side of the road, was not at all a common sight for people who lived on the very street that I grew up in. Agostino sat across from me, his eyes looking over the various Styrofoam containers of food that Mam' Ruby had placed on our table.

I could tell it wasn't really his cup of tea since the food was pap (kind of porridge made from maize meal), mogodu (tripe & intestines), tlhakwana (cow heels) and maotwana (chicken feet). Quite honestly, the African cuisine was an acquired taste but it was definitely not too easy on the eyes and neither was it a good smell, but I thoroughly enjoyed the food.

Mme Ruby's was a place that I ate at, a lot. Her food was the best and it was always made with love and care. She was also a drinking buddy of my mum's and in many ways, a close family friend. There were a lot of good memories from this spot.

I tried to stop laughing but I couldn't. Agostino's silent reaction was all that I needed to witness to know exactly what he was thinking; "what the fuck is this?" "stop! I'm going to pee on myself!" I struggled to finish the sentence as I placed my hand over my mouth, and tears escaped my eyes as I clutched the side of my stomach because it was beginning to hurt. "you said you wanted to try it!" I tried to argue in between hearty laughs.

He looked at me, his lips stretching into a small smile. "I'll try..." he trailed off, his eyes looking back at the food. His curly hair was pulled back into a neater style- he never tied his hair but he always managed to perfectly style it in a way that it didn't get in the way of his movements.

There were a few curly strands of hair that were rebellious but I think he allowed it because I commented on how it made him look better and begged him not to slick all the hair back. He was wearing a black Dolce & Gabbana suit that was covered in intricate lace designs that must have cost a pretty penny. He had the first two buttons of his shirt undone, and a golden chain around his neck. The were gold rings on his fingers, the most prominent being a gold ring with a large red ruby stone in the middle, placed on his left middle finger. But I think it must be a thing of status.

We were matching, both dressed in black. I was wearing a black Versace pantsuit with a pleated double breasted blazer. However, I wasn't wearing anything beneath the blazer, letting the slight plunge neckline of the blazer, reveal the beautiful diamond necklace that Agostino had gifted me last night when we arrived in South Africa. My hair was pulled back into a low ponytail and I had light makeup on.

We had just come from visiting my mum and grandma's graves, and while it had been emotional, it felt like a weight had been lifted off my shoulders now that I had the chance to visit them. I didn't cry too much, I just shed a tear or two, and spoke to my mum, cleaning around her gravestone and placing the expensive flowers that Agostino had bought. By the time we left the graveyard, their once empty graves were covered in the most flowers and it made me feel at ease.

"I'm kidding, don't worry. Mme Ruby is bringing over some wors (sausage) and red meat, and it's BBQed. That's what you Americans say, right?" I asked him for confirmation as I pulled the food that was on the table towards my direction, seeing Mme Ruby walk towards us with the tray filled with hot and saucy braaied meat. She smiled at me when we made eye contact before she set the things down.

Mme Ruby was 4 '10 and round, with four prominent beard hairs that had grown over the years that she chose not to get rid of. I hated them, because every time that she looked at me and spoke to me, all I could pay attention to was those beard hairs. She was a strict woman, but in order to run the business she does which was restaurant by day, and the towns hotspot Tavern by night- you just had to be. "dankie, ma (thank you, ma)."

"Alright, ngwanaka (Alright, my child)." She said with a soft tone as she quickly walked away, not wanting to stay too long. I couldn't blame her, Agostino's presence was heavy and he wasn't exactly being all too friendly, but then again, when was he? He hadn't said a word to her, just stared at her and even when I tried to catch up with her once she saw me and she started crying, he wasn't all too happy about the long conversation and told her to do what she's supposed to do. I apologised sheepishly to the woman and asked her to leave us alone.

"I used to come here all the time with my mum. The food is really affordable, and whenever my mum would feel lazy to cook, or my grandma was too tired. They would just send me to get some food and a couple of beers." I smiled at the fond memories, rolling up my sleeves as I began to eat my food with my hands. I looked at the cheap beer bottles that Agostino was opening up for us, thanking him when he handed me my own. "I remember this one time," I began to laugh, the memories of this place coming back tenfold. "my cousin, Promise, came to visit me for the December holidays."

I began to drone on, telling Agostino about the eventful night when I tried to sneak out with my cousin by jumping out of the window of my flat that was five storeys above ground. And as common sense would expect, we both ended up plummeting to the ground and had to be rushed to the hospital because we had broken quite a few bones.

"Good times." I said as I looked at Agostino.

It felt good to be home. I hadn't realised just how much I missed it. I missed everything about where I came from. The comforting sight of the near-run down flats where people hung their washing on their windows, the loitering of groups of young boys, the whistling of drunken men as they swore at the invisible people troubling them, the sound of three different songs being played all at once by different people. The sound of plastic and lousy scooters that kids played with, the yelling of mother's who were still dressed in nightgowns even though it was the afternoon.

I couldn't believe that I had left all of this behind and I was now with some Capo of the Italian mafia.

How does that even happen?

I tilted my head at Agostino, watching him and taking him in. At this point in my life, he was all that I knew, and all that I understood. I wondered why there was a sense of almost comfort when it came to him. Don't get me wrong, I am deathly afraid of the man. He has shown me that he is a monster. However, there are moments that I'm not proud of. Moments when my body and heart betray me, moments when I find myself placing my head on his chest, or intertwining our fingers together.

Maybe he has brainwashed me and I don't even realise it.

Sometimes, I think that the only reason that I feel like this about him is because I need someone, and at this point my mind, body and soul, would simply accept anyone who claimed to "want" me or love me. I had no one, and even though I had Alessandro at some point, I could see how he treated his other daughters- the love and care came naturally, whereas when it came to me he was always nervous and unsure. With Agostino, I was his choice. I felt like I was his number one, there was no hesitation, no unsurety- he knew what he wanted.

I needed help.

"You know," I said, bringing the beer bottle to my lips and drinking the cheap liquor. Agostino had spoiled me, I no longer enjoyed it as much as I used to now that I was used to his expensive liquor, however, the beer felt nostalgic. With one sip, I could remember lounging here with my mum on a random Sunday, drinking and imagining how life could turn out for me.

"I always wanted to go to New York," I found myself saying, wiping the corners of my mouth with the serviette.

"To sing?" he said more than asked and I raised an eyebrow.

"Yeah...how did you know that?" I asked him. I don't know why I'm so surprised, I'm sure he already knows all there is to know about me.

He looked up from his food and at me, his grey eyes holding my own and there was a jolt of need that coursed through my body and settled in the pools of my lower abdomen at the simple look. I didn't wait for him to respond, I just smiled and nodded my head, continuing, "my mum and I would sit here every now and then, and I would tell her about how...about how someday I would pursue my dream of becoming an opera singer and perform at some theatre in New York City." I could just picture my mum's proud and excited smile whenever we would talk about this. We would sit for hours and just dream, dream of making it out of this place and moving on to see the world. Looking back now, I don't think I was ever happier than when I was living here.

We never really see how the beginning is the best part.

"New York, New York," I sang in the same way my mother would chant whenever I would show her the online pictures or videos of theatres in New York, or opera singers performing. "she was really my biggest fan."

I sighed, placing my hands beneath my chin and resting my chin on my fists. I couldn't break away from Agostino's gaze. He held my eyes, his face expressionless, never really giving anything away, but goodness he would sit like that for hours and listen to me talk. I would drone on and on about the most useless of things and he would just stare at me, and when I was done, he would stand, kiss me on the forehead and leave to go to work or do whatever the hell he does, as long as its not to me- as selfish and heartless as that may sound.

"She saw the best in me, told me that I was the best opera singer she's ever heard in her life. It's funny because she didn't understand opera, not for a long time, but even though she didn't understand, she would always give me that R50 (Rand) for a taxi so that I could attend my lessons, and she would show up for my performances." I loved opera, with all there was within me. But I wasn't too sure that I could sing again, not after the incident. I hadn't tried though. I was too afraid of being disappointed. I reached my hand over the table, taking Agostino's hand in my own. His hand was large and swallowed mine whole but I loved to play with it, spinning the rings on his fingers, tracing the lines in his palm, feeling his skin...all of that. "thank you for today," I said earnestly, smiling at him, "I really missed home, and you allowed me to have the full experience. I couldn't have asked for a better day."

He brought my hand to his lips and kissed each individual knuckle before his thumb traced the back of my hand, "qualsiasi cosa per te, la mia colomba autunnale. (anything for you, my Autumn dove)."

CHAPTER 13

I'm not really sure what I was expecting, but the pin drop silence and the downcast eyes was just not one of them. I thought that Alessandro and his family would at least pretend to be happy to see me, since the last time that we were together things had been going so well. We sat around the simple dinner table, no one really saying anything, and none of them met my eye. I just wanted things to go back to normal- I wanted to hear Greta drone on about her day, and Alessandro make bad jokes about the food that we were eating, and Gabriela to roll her eyes and complain under her breath about how he was the world's worst comedian. But there was none of that.

In fact, the moment that the Rolls Royce Cullinan had come to a stop outside the home, they were standing outside, as if waiting for the First Lady. I guess, I should have better understood and interpreted their uncomfortable and fearful faces, even though they had nothing to be scared of. It was just me.

I placed a smile on my face, taking it upon myself to start off some conversation, "so how have things been?" I asked in an unsure tone, speaking Italian since I was beginning to better understand the language.

Alessandro was the one who spoke up, "well, they have been good." He answered me and even though it was a good answer- great, actually. It hurt to hear that since I had been gone, things seemed to be going well. They had yet to tell me that they had missed me, or even give me a proper hug without their bodies being rigid and afraid in my arms.

It seemed as though I were the plague, and something told me that it was because of the company that I was keeping. Being around Agostino really tainted you and everything that you were. He was poison, seeping into every pore, every thought, every doubt, every person and spoiling you for everyone else. Suddenly his words "...I'll take it all, until I'm the only one left, until I'm all that you have." Hit way to hard. I didn't even have to attempt to escape in order for his words to be true, because sitting at the table where we once used to sit and laugh, talk about our days and never run out of words; the silence was resounding.

I was tired of the silence. I was met with silence everywhere that I went, everywhere that I sat, everywhere that I stepped- pure silence. No one talked to me, not the staff at the house, not the guards, and Agostino was busy most of the time. I missed the booming laughter from Alessandro when he would "accidently" tip over the bowl of peas and say "oh no, I pea'd on the table!" and bring himself to tears with what he thought was a phenomenal joke, while I would giggle at the way that he never seemed to care what we thought and would just let himself be. I missed the way that Greta would talk my ear off about school and the guys that liked her, or the way that Aurora would tell me about the strange dreams she had of talking chickens and dancing goats, or the way that Matteo would draw the world's worst scribbles and say that it was me.

I was about to scream. If someone didn't talk to me, I was sure that I was going to lose it.

"Greta, how was school?" I chose to say, hoping that me saying her name would encourage her to talk.

She didn't look up from her plate, "fine." She answered me shortly, and I dropped my fork, feeling myself reach my limit. I cleared my throat, suddenly losing my appetite and the lasagne no longer looking and tasting that amazing.

"I...I can't..." I croaked out, standing to my feet and pushing my chair back, hearing it loudly screech against the tiled floors. They all were silent, but I had their attention because for the first time in the evening, they looked at me. However, this time, I didn't want to look at them so I walked away, and made my way to the front door. When I stepped out of the front door, the two men posted at either side of the door turned their heads to look at me but I walked through them, making my way to the other end of the patio and leaning against the wooden railings that would cause lots of splinters.

I shut my eyes, letting the night air nip at my skin and tried to calm down my breathing. I heard the sound of the front door opening and closing, but I didn't really care because I was trying to collect myself. After a few moments I suddenly felt a presence beside me, and I opened my eyes and turned my head, looking up at the man that was my father. He looked at me, but he couldn't even hold eye contact with me, his eyes trailing away and looking down or looking behind me. My throat was tight and suddenly, it didn't help that I was trying to recollect myself, "you won't even look at me…" I found myself saying in a broken whisper. "look at me, Alessandro…." I pleaded, needing to be seen.

I watched as he visibly swallowed, his brows furrowing and his expression becoming solemn. "I can't…" he told me, his voice sounding strained as he tried to hold my eyes but he looked away. However, I felt him wrap an arm around me and bring me into his body. I placed my face in his chest and cried, letting out all that I had been holding in. Suddenly, I cried because I had been so silly as to make eye contact with a man like Agostino when I was still a waitress, I cried because I had so excitedly prepared myself for a date with him. I cried because he had raped me, I cried because of all the things that I had seen in the basement, then I cried because Agostino told me that I could never leave. I cried because I tried to run, but Agostino caught me and put me through hell, and I cried because despite all that, I somehow felt that Agostino was the only person who didn't look past me or through me, but instead at me.

Alessandro, wordlessly held me, his big arms around me and the comfortable pot belly served as a kind of comfort only a father could provide. For the first time in a long while, I felt safe and protected, in the shield that came with a father's love. I could hear his heart beat, hear the way that he breathed, and I could feel the deathly tight grip around me as he pulled me impossibly closer.

I cried until the tears slowed to a stop, and when I pulled back from his chest and looked at him, I felt like a little child.

His eyes held a gentleness in them that I had seen directed towards his other children, but never towards me. My heart soared, and suddenly my hiccups came to a still and my arms wrapped tighter around his stomach.

I suddenly felt another pair of arms wrap around me and a bed of curls invade my senses, and I knew that it was Greta. She and her outrageous yet beautiful hair was always a sight, "oh, I love a group hug!" she suddenly exclaimed with joy as she buried her face in my neck and I lightly laughed, turning my face away from her hair that was coming into my nostrils. We stood in each others arms for some time, swaying side to side, breathing each other's scents in and I thoroughly enjoyed the moment.

"I'm scared, Delaney." She said in a whisper, speaking into our bodies, disguising her words away from the guards. "I wish you could come back home…" she trailed off but we all knew that the only way that I was ever going to come back home was in a casket. There was no other way around it. "the whole town's talking about you…talking about the woman that the dono della morte has taken. None of the other women lasted this long." She was whispering it to me than to my father whose head had been turned the other way and Greta and I were face to face with each other, speaking in whispers.

"There were others?" I asked her and Greta gave a small nod.

"They were with him for a week, and suddenly, there was a funeral and there the family of whatever woman it was- having a closed casket funeral. Never any longer than a week or two, not to mention the months that you have spent with him." she paused her eyes gazing into my own in a way that was filled with panic, concern, suspicion- all the sorts, "the Italian mafia is coming to Merton," she relayed to me, "and if the Italian mafia don travels all the way from Italy to Merton once in the 15 years that the dono della morte has been running his business, it means one thing and one thing alone..."

"What's that?"

"A wedding."

CHAPTER 14

As I walked through the home I could hear the sound of music, and upon closer attention, the song that was playing softly over the speakers throughout the home was Back to Black by Amy Winehouse. I almost winced at the memories that hit me like a brick to the face.

This song started it all; specifically, the first glance that Agostino and I shared and it had led to something bigger and darker than any of us could ever imagine. I can't ever imagine having to listen to this song ever again, or even enjoy it as much as I used to; and I used to adore Amy Winehouse. But I despised the song now because it was tainted and associated with Agostino, which can never be a good thing. Much like myself, ironically.

I slowly strolled through the hallways, the Dior handbag dangled carelessly from my fingers, hitting my ankle occasionally as I massaged my neck, feeling the weight of the expensive diamond around my neck. My body was adorned in jewellery, Agostino loved to put diamonds and real gold on me. A pair of gold and busy earrings dangled from my ears, jingling with movements, showing off the jewels that adorned it. My hair had been pulled back into the perfect messy bun, however, following the hug that I shared with Greta and Alessandro, it was simply messy now. My hair was falling out of the bun, and I didn't care to either undo the bun and let my hair be free, nor fix up the bun since I would be able to do so. I was tired and I didn't care for my appearance any longer.

I was wearing a Chanel glittered tweed black and gold dress that reached mid-thigh and its sleeves reached just above my elbows, allowing some movement since they weren't skin tight. My wrists were covered in jewellery, several diamond bracelets that seemed to get more expensive, a Rolex watch covered in diamonds and gold bangles that made a noise whenever I approached. Quite honestly, I seemed like the kind of wealthy housewife I always aspired to be deep down inside. The jewellery, the designer clothes, a man with more money than he cared for, judging by the way that he gave me a fat envelope filled with cash to give to Alessandro- which Alessandro dared not to decline when I handed him the fat brown envelope.

I leaned against the door with my left arm and looked into the room finding Agostino sitting on his office table, looking down at a picture frame. He seemed to be lost in whatever it was that he was looking at, I wondered what it was that had captured him so much so, that I'm not really sure that he knew I was standing here. He was always so aware of his surroundings, so aware of everything going on that by now he would have called my name. I took this moment to take him in. He was wearing a pair of black dress pants and a black shirt that had the first two buttons undone. His tie that had been so neatly tied around his neck before I left was now dangling on either side of his neck. His hair was neat as always, and he held a cigar to his lips. He was a lover of Cuban cigars, but never around me, and I partially wondered if it was because he knew that I didn't like when people smoked in front of me.

I straightened up, and walked into the room, keeping my gaze on him. He seemed to be aware of my presence now because he looked up and those dark grey eyes collided with my own. I couldn't help but smile, tilting my head, "what are you looking at?" I asked him, approaching him and he dangled the picture frame.

He turned it around and faced me and the face that I met was my own. I walked closer to him, and took the picture frame in my hands and looked it over, looking at the woman in the picture. The picture had been taken a few weeks ago, back when we were on his private island. I was wearing a vibrant green grass skirt that I had begged Agostino to make for me from scratch, and in the picture I was holding up two coconuts to my breasts laughing with my hair that was being blown by the wind. A flower crown covered the front part of my hair, keeping it out of my face and giving me a more youthful appearance, and the beach could be seen behind me. I felt a small smile grow on my face, able to feel the distant memory of sand between my toes and the fresh and humid air.

"I love the beach," I said with a smile as I handed Agostino the picture back and I watched as he placed it on the corner of his desk. His desk was almost empty, except for the computer and two neatly stacked files and a landline. Seeing my vibrant picture seemed so out of place for the dark and masculine office.

I placed the Dior handbag on the table and found myself wrapping my arms around Agostino's shoulders and letting out a heavy breath. "did you survive without me?" I asked with a light laugh, as I began to play with his hair behind his neck.

"Barely," he entertained me, wrapping his arm around my waist and bringing me closer before he placed a kiss on the top of my head. Peering into his eyes, I could never tell what he was thinking or feeling. Greta's words ran through my mind, playing over like a broken record. I was comfortable around Agostino, doing things willingly that I thought I would never do, however, my body just did. But despite how comfortable I was around him, I never forgot what he was capable of. There was always that fear when I had to ask him something, fearing for my life and what he would do to me. I watched what I said when I was around him, afraid for my and my family's life.

I wanted so much to ask him if there had been other women before me, and if so, how many had they been. A part of me wanted to know what they had done, but I figured they tried to escape or he simply got bored of them and took them down to his basement. I pitied them, but in a way also envied them, for he was still playing around with me until he got bored; while they were finally done and at peace- depending on the kind of life they lived, of course. I wanted to ask about the so called Mafia don making his way to Merton, and I wondered if there was a wedding...could it be mine? Would he keep it a secret from me? When was he going to tell me? Or was everyone else wrong and there would be no wedding?

I began to sway side to side naturally, the song back to black came to an end and I was suddenly met with the familiar sound of Beyonce's XO and a huge smile crossed my lips. I knew this playlist like the back of my hand, I blasted it throughout the home every other day. It was my feel good playlist and there was absolutely nothing you could say or do that would in any way interrupt my blasting this playlist. And no matter how many times I played the songs, I never tired of them because they put me in a good mood. "this is my favourite song in the whole wide world!" I excitedly told Agostino, grabbing his hands and forcing him to his feet, forcing him to dance with me.

My sudden tired body came to life as I excitedly moved to the song, singing out the words and forcing Agostino to spin me around even though it was obvious that he did not care for dancing or for the song as much as I did. I grinned ear to ear, pulling off the kind of dance moves that I did whenever this song came on, forcing Agostino to participate, but the straight expression on his face loosened before he let out a chuckle when I tried to do the robot. He shook his head at me, taking the Cuban cigar out of his mouth, turning and walking back to his desk.

I laughed too, my hair having come undone and now using it as I tried to whip my hair back and forth, so much so that I made myself dizzy and I stumbled to the point where I was about to fall but Agostino caught my body. My body lay in his arms as though he had dipped me, and once that I calmed from the outrageous laughter that came from the pits of my stomach and caught my breath, I found him simply looking at me. "what?" I asked him, my hand on his shoulder, my body still dipped and Agostino still holding me in his arms, in a way that let me know that I would never hit the ground if he was ever around me.

"Just taking you in," he told me as he lifted me up and I continued to dance to next song, not caring for what he said but knowing very well that he was watching me as I danced around his office.

CHAPTER 15

"Why do you keep tossing and turning?" I heard Agostino's voice break through the silent room. I gasped, surprised that I had woken him up with my tossing and turning since it was dead in the night and I wasn't able to sleep. I bit my bottom lip and held my breath, trying to remain still as I responded to him.

"Sorry," I whispered, bringing the blanket to my chin and gripping onto its edges as I stared at Agostino's face. His eyes were still closed, and if he hadn't said a word, I would have still believed that he was fast asleep. "sorry." I repeated.

He was silent for a moment, "what's on your mind?" he finally asked, as though he already knew what I was thinking or had studied me so much so, that he knew if I was tossing and turning it was because something was on my mind.

"Why would you think I have something on my mind?" I retaliated, even though I knew that he was right. I did have something on my mind. Greta's words were coursing through my brain in waves and I was so anxious to find out the truth. But I knew that there was no way that I could say anything to

Agostino without him hurting me in the end. I didn't want to go through the glass saga again, because I can guarantee that my next punishment will be even more severe. And I'm afraid that if I were to be punished again, it would end with me in a casket or in a mental hospital...even worse, in his basement.

He opened his eyes, and glared directly into my own as though he had no time for my nonsense. I pursed my lips awkwardly but knew that he wanted to know what it was that I was thinking about. "I'm scared to say..." I finally whispered out, my mind suddenly getting flashbacks of the gruesome pain of having to chew and swallow glass. Even though it was dark in his room, my eyes had adjusted to the darkness since I had spent the better half of the night very much so wide awake, with my eyes bouncing off the walls and trying my best to imagine fake scenarios to go to sleep.

He smoothed his fingers over his eyebrows and let out a heavy breath as though I were a toddler who refused to give him a break. "speak, my dove, there won't be consequences for now." He told me but it did little to calm me.

"Okay, promise me that you won't get mad," I pleaded softly, my eyes peering into his, hoping for once that those grey orbs would reveal a little something but they were blank as always. His face straightened even further at my statement and I knew that I was playing on his nerves, and that wasn't a good thing. "okay, okay, sorry." I nervously swallowed, "it's just that... you know, I was wondering if, like...you know, there were...you know...other girlfriends you had in your life, or other women, you know...somewhat...maybe, like me?" I stuttered out, struggling to form the words and let them out of my throat that was fighting with me to speak.

My throat unlike my tongue knew better. It fought against me, begging me not to talk with the way my airways tightened, and it made it hard to breathe- let alone talk.

"Yes," he responded smoothly and simply, his words factual and to the point. There was no hesitation, no nerves, just his bland attitude at times. "I have been with other women before you, I'm a man." Well obviously, that may be true but unlike other men, he was practically butchering us, from the inside to the outside.

"Did you...did you treat them like me?" I continued. One of my other thoughts were whether he had treated them like me. Did he treat them better? Did he treat them worse? Of course it was worse, they were all dead. According to what Greta had to say.

"No, you have it easier. They never truly captured my attention any longer than a few days before they simply got on my nerves. It was more entertaining when I took them to the basement, more than it was to stay in their company. There was nothing of substance in previous women, and those who tried to pretend that there was, again, went to the basement." He responded as though his words made all the more sense and it was obvious what had to be done. A chill ran down my naked spine. Suddenly I wanted to detangle the leg that I had wrapped around his legs, my body having being basked in the afterglow of sex. I just wanted to get as far away from him as possible, but I dared not make a move.

"All of them?" I croaked out, my eyes wide and nervous as I looked into his. "if that was their fate...then what will be mine?"

I asked him, wondering if that was what was going to happen to me. "will I end up in the basement?" I don't know why I was asking something that seemed so blatantly obvious to me.

Agostino was silent before I felt his hand make its way onto my face and push the bonnet that I was wearing off my forehead and closer to my hairline. His fingers then traced the outline of my face before he spoke up, "sometimes I'm tempted to take you there even when you haven't done anything wrong." His words caused me to grip onto the sheets tighter and my heart to begin pounding fearfully in my chest, "but then I'll look at you, in your eyes, and I can't go through with it. Then I go from the desire to hurt you, to holding you and listening to whatever boring story that you're excited to tell me about."

I licked my bottom lip, before I ran my top row teeth over the lip, grazing it in thought. I didn't know how to feel about his words. "why do you like to hurt people?" I asked him. It was obvious that he was mentally challenged, but that's something I would never say out loud. I needed to hear what he believed his reasoning was to do what he did to other people.

"Because it's what I do and it's how I was raised. It's in my blood, my grandfather taught it to my father, my father taught it to me, and someday, I will teach it to my own sons."

A sick man like Agostino wanted children? Some people should never be able to bring innocent life into this world only to corrupt it and turn it into a monster. It was strange to imagine Agostino as a child, it seemed as though he had been a monster and adult all his life. I'm sure he came out of the womb this tall and built and ready to hurt innocent people for no reason. "were they all in the mafia?"

"Yes."

"Will you ever get married someday? Is there even marriage in the mafia?"

He remained silent and looked at me before he turned back onto his back and looked up at the ceiling. "go to bed, my dove, that's enough questions for the night." He told me, and I watched as he closed his eyes. I watched the gentle rise of his chest, my eyes looking over every inch of his face. Even in his sleep he seemed like a Greek god; mighty and handsome.

I followed his action and turned on my back and looked up at the ceiling. He hadn't answered my question about marriage but he didn't need to because his silence was answer enough. For once, he didn't have something to say and it made me wonder which of the following reasons it was. Could he believe that he will never marry because no woman has ever held his interest? Or maybe that had been his belief for a long time but things gradually change with time and he feels that he's ready for it? Could it be that I was the one who made him think like that? Made him believe in marriage? That could possibly go against all that he was taught from birth by his father and the men in the mafia.

It didn't help that he said that he wanted to hurt me and there were moments when he wanted to take me to the basement but he didn't because my eyes distracted him. Would I live the rest of my life afraid that whatever he sees in my eyes will one day disappear and he won't be able to fight the urge to take me to the basement? This isn't the kind of life that I wanted to live, nevertheless be stuck in. I can't imagine ever having to bear the children of a monster like Agostino.

Chapter 16

Something was going on, I could just feel it. There was a sickening feeling of dread in the pits of my stomach as I stood in the centre of my dressing room, surrounded by gowns and makeup of all kinds, having several professionals busy with my appearance. That wasn't what was strange- I was used to it by now, I was used to the help that wasn't all that necessary when I had to get ready. I had a makeup artist who would spend the greater part of the morning always making sure that I looked flawless throughout all the days, and a hair stylist who knew the way that I liked my hair to be handled, along with a stylist who put me in clothes that were to die for.

However, there was a certain way that they seemed to make sure that I looked better than usual today. Which is saying a lot because every time that they get me ready, I seem to look more perfect than the previous. There was a level of concentration on their faces that wasn't there before. I stood, letting the stylist slip the expensive looking brown leather trench coat over the brown leather midi dress that I wore. The dress was beautiful, it was a fitted, sleeveless, mid-length dress that was open on either side of my legs, exposing my legs and thighs. It hugged me as though it were second skin, the brown leather almost meshing with my skin tone. They paired the look with a pair of Fendi brown leather knee-high boots that added five inches to my height.

My hair was pulled into a high ponytail, making sure that not a strand was out of place and they added extensions to my hair to increase its volume and length. They had just redyed my hair, making sure that the ginger coloured hair was fresh and popped out much more than usual. My makeup wasn't heavy, it usually never was, however it was done in such a way that it created a colder look. It made me feel as though, I really did belong on the arm of Agostino, because the fox eyes that the makeup artist had created on my face made me seem fiercer as though I could take on the runway and own it. The look was dewy and finished well, and my lip was a toned brown that matched my skin tone and my outfit. A pair of large diamond studs dangled from my earrings, not too overpowering, but enough to let you know that they were as expensive as they were heavy.

I had a different necklace around my neck today, this one was heavier and larger, with more diamonds all around it. My nails were clear and long, having the perfect coffin shape at the end, and completing my look of sophistication. The trench coat was long, and reached just below my ankles. Suddenly the feeling of dread worsened at the remembrance of Greta's words.

Could it be?

Could today be the day when his mafia family arrived?

It would explain so much. It would explain why the staff was running through the halls as though they couldn't get enough done on time.

I looked outside, looking out at the cloudy weather, feeling as solemn as it. Even the earth seemed to be feeling the dread that I was feeling. The door to the room opened and Agostino stood on the other side. He was dressed well, as always. He wore a pair of black dress pants with a black turtleneck, and he wore a black coat over, one that was all the way buttoned up. His hands were covered in black leather gloves, but something told me that it wasn't because it was cold. Atop his curly hair, was a black leather 1930's cap and a lit cigar between his lips.

He took the cigar out of his mouth, and the women in the room left quietly and quickly as I looked up at him. "what's going on?" I asked him, accepting the hand that he graced me with as I began to descend from the podium that allowed me to view myself from all angles as I was getting dressed.

"Some very important people are going to be here, my Autumn dove," he told me, his eyes running over every inch of my face as though it were the first time that he was seeing me. I straightened up, tilting my head to the side and my eyebrows furrowed in confusion.

"How important?" I chose to say and I saw him let out a smirk, as though my question amused him.

"Important enough to get me to wear this hat," he chuckled out and even though I wanted to marvel at how he had graced me with one of those rare occasions of a laugh, I couldn't shake the feeling that something big was coming my way. "you need to watch your mouth today. You don't speak unless you're spoken to and if you so much as hold eye contact for longer than three seconds, I'll be the one who delivers a lethal shot to your head, understand?" his Italian was flawless and smooth, his words delivering a message that made me grip onto his hand in fear. There was a seriousness in those orbs that I was much too used to.

"Okay..." I mumbled out, whispering low in fear that if I raised my voice, it would upset him.

You know when you're In the presence of someone powerful? You seem to get that aura, that shift in the air, the way people's backs seem to straighten impossibly rigid, the way that said man entered with an air of dominance and arrogance? There was a certain level of power that emitted off of Agostino, that I cannot deny, however the man who walked into Agostino's underground bar was a man that I could tell simply called the shots.

Remove whatever romanticised version of a don that you have in your mind and realise that in real life, mafia don's are not as they are written to be in romantic fairy tale books. The don was a short man, shorter than me at his height of 5'3 and fat in a way that told you he cared very little for his outer appearance because he had all that he could desire. He was partially balding and what remained of his hair was oily and sticking to his skin in an unappetising or appealing way. He wore a pair of black pants held together by a belt beneath his potbelly, and a plain black golf shirt that he had tucked into his pants. He had two golden chains around his neck and there were several watches and rings on his hands. He entered the room surrounded by an army of men, all of whom were taller than him, but you knew that they bowed down to him.

He rubbed his hands together, entering the bar, and the army of men immediately spreading to the corners of the room as he waved his hand dismissively. He looked at Agostino, his beady brown eyes paying attention to Agostino as a drunken grin spread across his face, "Tino! Tino," he called joyfully as he spread his arms wide and walked to Agostino, hugging Agostino who made no move to return the hug and simply stood there. He laughed boisterously at Agostino's response, "you never liked to touch, I can see how that has remained the same." He spoke in a heavily accented Italian.

"God, do you only get taller? Look at you, look at Merton and all that you have done. That's good, I knew that you were a good choice, the best from all of your other useless cousins. You know," he began conversation, but paused midway and looked blankly around the room, "I'm in a bar and I don't have a fucking drink in my hand, whose throat should I slit?" he said casually, his words containing ice and a promise. In seconds there was a glass of whiskey with ice that was placed in his hands and a cigar that they held up to his lips for him to smoke and enjoy. "you know that Matteo, I thought he was smarter, I gave him Miami, told him to take care of it. And what does he do? He fucks it all up, ruins it for me and all that I have built.

See this is what I get for hiring my brother, that fat fuck. You should see him, he loves tacos too much that it's making him fucking Mexican and fucking with his brain." He shrugged his shoulders, "eh, eh, you're the only one, I tells you Tino, I've got big things planned for you." He completed in broken English.

He hadn't even glanced towards me, but Agostino's words ran through my mind and I dared not to look at him. The only time I had happened to glance was when he had entered the room. I looked down at his feet, standing a few feet away from him and Agostino in silence, hoping that today wouldn't end in my murder. I don't think he even noticed me or if he did, he chose not to address it but I spoke too soon because I felt his attention shift from whatever they had been discussing to me.

"Is this the woman?" I heard him ask, watching him move his body weight from one leg to another as he stood there. I heard Agostino agree, and he extended his hand for me to accept. I placed my hand in Agostino's and let him pull me closer, making sure not to make eye contact with the don. "okay…okay," he murmured in Italian, his voice dropping lower, "your eyes working okay, Tino? She's black, she's not Italian." I heard him say, his voice back to its normal tone of loud and boisterous. He was silent before he turned and looked around the room, "are you all seeing Tino's woman?" he asked the room, there was silence except for one of the men who agreed, the don seemed to notice him right away. "you seeing her? What do you think, eh?" he asked the man.

The man was silent, he was wearing a black suit much like the other men in the room. Except unlike Agostino's men, they didn't wear black shades. "she's not Italian," the man responded and I heard the don hum, before the don looked around the room and chuckled, before he looked at Agostino.

"Did you hear that? He said she's not Italian," he repeated and my heart raced, my cheeks flushing as I stood there, feeling targeted for my skin tone. I partially wondered why Agostino wasn't saying anything in my defence but then again he probably couldn't stand up to the don or else he would be killed. "somebody give me a gun," I heard the don say and I froze, gripping onto Agostino's hand in fear for my life. This was it, I was going to die.

One of the men stepped forward with a gun and when the don took it into his hand, he raised it towards the man who spoke and shot him in his kneecaps, "you dare talk about Tino's woman? You dare speak about my cousin and his woman? Piece of shit, I'll shove you back in your mother's vagina for fucking listening to my conversation and adding your fucking cheap opinion" I heard the don snap at the man, shaking his head.

The man was screaming in agony but the don sighed and handed the gun back to his other man, "take him to Tino's basement. See, Tino, never say I don't love you, I brought you a little pet." He had a new glass of whiskey in his hand and my eyes were snapped shut as I tried to calm my breathing, seeing the pool of blood as I heard the men begin to drag the other man away. "I figure she's something special if you picked up the phone and told me about her. I can tell she's scared though. What? She's hasn't seen blood before? She needs to get used to it if she's with you. What's your name, black lady?" he asked me in Italian, turning his attention towards me.

I swallowed nervously and looked to Agostino, seeing if he wanted me to respond now. I saw his slight nod of approval, "Delaney Dardan." I responded, trying to sound in the least bit unshaken but I was. He seemed to be so jolly one second, then talkative, and then a murderer. He was difficult to understand how to behave around him.

"Look me in the eye, Delaney," he paused, slurping on his whiskey, as I kept my eyes to his chest. He extended his arms as though he were welcoming me, "we're going to be family." He laughed.

CHAPTER 17

Agostino didn't seem to be the spontaneous type of man, however this morning he pulled one over my eyes. I thought that we were going to be spending the day with his mafia family whom had all arrived and I had been introduced. All of them looked over the fact that I was obviously not Italian and simply paid more attention to him than I. The only one who ever really paid any attention to me was the don and he would usually be asking a random question, that didn't necessarily make me uncomfortable but it was obvious that he was rarely around black people so he asked those uncomfortable kind of question that were borderline comical.

After breakfast, Agostino told me that we had somewhere to be but we would be back soon. He had his private airport in his backyard, and there were two other planes parked (which belonged to his uncle and his cousin) right next to his. We hopped onto his black Gulfstream G280, my body and attitude indifferent to the luxury plane because I had become so accustomed to it, and it practically felt like a car because of how frequently Agostino travelled.

I wasn't all too sure where I thought he would be taking us, but I figured it was for business and he had something to attend to. Or it was like those days when he would take me shopping, however when the plane landed in an airport where a helicopter awaited us- I finally realised- when we were lifted into the air and I could see all throughout the city- that he had brought me to New York. "oh my God!" I gasped, turning my head to look at Agostino excitedly, "are we in New York?" I squealed, even though the statue of liberty was within eye shot and I could see the empire state building in the distance as we rode around in the helicopter.

Agostino looked at me and nodded as I jumped around in my seat and continued to look out. My hair flipped widely with the feel of the wind against my face as my eyes looked around in awe at a city that I had only seen in movies. Listen, I was no stranger to the big city. However, you can't deny the magic that is New York City. It's in all of the movies and anything to do with luxury, fun, work, gambling, dinner reservations, celebrities, wealth- all of the sorts- New York was always in the midst. I couldn't believe that I was in the greatest city in the world, not entirely my belief, but hey, that's what they campaign it to be.

"I'm in New York right now!" I squealed, watching as the helicopter landed on the capital H on the ground, safely and gently. I took off my headpiece, and let Agostino help me out of the helicopter as I adjusted the dress that I wore which was a show stopping black number that put all of my previous outfits to shame. The dress was a custom Givenchy floor-length dress that had an off the shoulder neckline and was sleeveless.

It was a mermaid style dress that clung onto every bit of skin and the illusion blended well with my skin tone to make the black sheer lace material seem as though it had been grown onto me. The top of the dress, around my neckline was covered in dramatic feathers, creating a pattern around the plunging neckline between my breasts, all the way to below my ribcage. The sides of the dress, along my stomach were exposed in the skin toned illusion that helped reveal my back in its entirety.

The back was completely open with the dress beginning right below my back dimples, just above my ass but in a way that was classy and sexy at the same time. There was a slit along my left thigh, showcasing my legs and making the dress trail behind me. There were feathers along the bottom of the dress as well, completing a look of sophistication, class and extravagance all in one with a pair of black Jimmy Choo heels. My hair had been done into voluminous curls, and it was just as dramatic as my dress.

"What are we doing here?" I asked Agostino, very much so taken aback by how he seemed to grow more handsome day by day. We were matching today. He wore a custom black Balenciaga suit, whose jacket was covered in the same black lace that my dress was made out of. His hair was pulled back in the way that it usually is and he was wearing less jewellery than normal. However, that didn't mean that his wrist wasn't adorned in an expensive Rolex watch and his fingers weren't covered in his three most important rings.

"You'll see," he answered me as he wrapped his arm around my waist and pulled me closer to his body as we entered the building that we had landed on and began walking down a set of stairs, carefully taking steps so that I wouldn't fall on my face and embarrass myself.

I don't know where I thought he was taking me, but moments later, there was no denying the familiar music playing in my ears to the kind of music that I was obsessed with. Opera. My eyes widened slightly and I looked at Agostino but he showed nothing, giving nothing away as always and as we continued to walk, I was finally able to recognise the Opera house where a woman I had always seemed to watch on YouTube stood before me, on a stage that I never thought I would see in this lifetime; Cecilia Bartoli. My gasp bordered on a scream as I stood there and looked at her in all of her glory, standing on that stage and performing "Caro mio ben". Her voice carried throughout the empty yet well lit opera house as though it sang to the angels.

I couldn't help the way that I began to get teary eyed as I stood in the presence of one of the world's greatest opera singers. I was in shock, wondering how the Italian woman could possibly be standing in front of me, her eyes looking into my own with a ghost of a smile on her face as she held her arms out and sang passionately. "how?" I croaked out in awe as I looked at Agostino, overwhelmed with joy as I threw myself at him and hugged him with all the strength that I had in me. "is this for me?" I didn't have to ask because I knew it was, but it was still amazing that he would even think to do such a thing for me.

He rubbed my back gently, "yes, my Autumn dove."

"I don't know what to say except that this is the best thing anyone has ever done for me," I said as I pulled from the hug and looked back at the stage, wiping away my tears of joy as I stood there with my hands over my heart, closing my eyes at the beautiful music that I could spend years simply listening to.

I stood there, taking my surroundings in. It felt like a dream. I was standing in front of Cecilia Bartoli in the Metropolitan Opera House, getting a private performance that I knew not many were too fortunate to witness.

"I'm glad you like it, la mia colomba autunnale," he began as he turned me towards him, placing his hands on either side of my waist and making me look up at him. His hands gently wiped at the remainder of my happy tears and I let out a genuine smile, nodding my head at his statement in agreement. His hand made its way around my neck, pulling me in for a gentle kiss, "all too often these days, I find myself doing things like this and putting in effort to bring this smile on your face." He caressed my cheek, his dark grey eyes not really reflecting the gentleness that his words held however I didn't expect much from him.

I placed my hands on his chest, wondering what this was about. "the truth is, Delaney," he finally said my name- for the first time. It was strange to hear him address me by name and not call me his Autumn dove which he affectionately done so. I wasn't too sure what to feel about it though, but I could feel the racing of my heart in my chest that pounded nervously, hanging onto every word, "my heart... it speaks when I'm with you and you alone, and it's never done that before. So," he let go of me and I watched as he reached into the inside of his jacket before he pulled out a black velvet box, and he proceeded to get down on one knee. "take this ring, and marry me." he wasn't asking me, he never really did and I suddenly realised what this was all for.

He brought me here to propose to me after the don and his family had given their approval. Greta was right, damn it, she was right. I had a feeling that Agostino wasn't the type who dragged out engagements either and the reason his family was here, was because there was going to be a wedding. Very obviously, my wedding.

But what could I do? Living with Agostino has taught me one thing and one thing alone, he called the shots, and he always gave you two choices; life or death. I wasn't ready to die yet, I was terrified of what came after. So I made my choice; life. I extended my hand in his direction and nodded my head, the smile extinct on my face as my eyes saddened at the sight of the big diamond that he placed on my finger that told me that there was no way that I was ever going to get away from him.

Not if he had anything to do with it.

CHAPTER 18

Looking at Alessandro right now- I knew that I didn't know the man well enough. He was my father, but he wasn't my dad. I can't say that I never wished to meet the man who fathered me, but the men that my mother brought around me, simply lessened the desire to have meet the man. Because I figured that my father was probably a married man that ditched my mother after he found out about her pregnancy and I was not in the least bit interested in meeting a man like that.

There was a look on Alessandro's face, a look of...morbid dread, as though his world had come crumbling down all around him and there was absolutely nothing that he could to save it. I had felt that too, because once upon time- what feels like a whole lifetime ago, but was only months ago- it had been me when I had been clutching onto my mother's deceased body, begging for her to come back because she was all that I had. I can't describe the feeling in words because there are no words in the dictionary to describe what I had felt in that moment...however, as I looked at Alessandro right now, that expression on his face and the glassy look in his eyes...that was it. That was the emotion.

Another part of me, the child part of me was happy to see that. Happy to see that my father could feel my pain. I had thought that with my mother's passing there would be no one to be there for me, no one who will care for me and no one who will shed a tear for me. Looking back now, I wish I had made more effort for Alessandro and I. I wish that we had created the kind of father-daughter relationship that I saw on TV, or hell, the very one that he had with his two other daughters (my half-sisters). Maybe if I had made a little more effort and wasn't so closed off or so depressed, I wouldn't have found myself running straight into the arms of Agostino.

I watched as Alessandro slowly buried his face in his hand, covering his face before he began to cry. He cried for me as though I were already dead and he was identifying my body or attending my funeral. His cries were the kind that made the hairs on the back of my neck stand, and the pipes of my throat to tighten around the ball that was forming. Tears stung the back of my eyes as I looked down at the heavy diamond ring around my finger, feeling as though I were carrying a curse.

The home was deathly silent- a complete contrast to how it had been when I had walked in- before telling them that Agostino had asked me to marry him, and invited them to the wedding that was taking place first thing tomorrow morning. They all suddenly turned deathly pale, even 6 year old Matteo. Without a word, they all stood, in silence, and Gabriela wrapped her arms around her daughters and son who began to silently cry, and took them out of the living room and locked herself and the kids in her bedroom. Alessandro sat there for what felt like forever, before he stood and walked to the kitchen, kicking over the stools around the island and punching several kitchen cabinets before he leaned against the counter.

"What have I done to deserve this?" he cried, shaking his head and removing his hand from his face as he looked up at the sky, as though directly speaking to God. "what have I done to deserve this?" his tone was full of heartbreak and despair, as though he were sincerely asking from the bottom of his heart.

I shut my eyes, begging myself not to cry but it was futile because I realised what this meant. This was a death sentence, Agostino would never let me go. This was my journey towards my death, and my family would only prepare themselves for the funeral. My hands began to tremble and I wanted to take the ring off my finger, God knows I wanted to rip it off my finger and fling it as far as I could. Instead, I cried, "Alessandro, please..." I begged him, "please help me get out of this. I don't know what to do. I need your help, please." I pleaded in the kind of desperation a dying mother would in front of her child.

I knew that there wasn't much that he could do, or anything at all. But he was my father, he had to know something. He had to be able to get me out of this because everyone else is powerless. My father is the only man on this earth who should be able to fight tooth and nail for me, who should be able to stand for me. I begged him because he was the only person that I had left in the world that I could turn to. "I don't know how," he responded despondently. "I don't know how to help you, Delaney, I don't know what to do. I don't know what to do." He repeated hopelessly as he suddenly threw himself onto the large fridge and gripped onto the sides of it, pressing his forehead against it.

"Please, anything, anything at all. I need you...dad, please." He shook his head, as though needing to rid my voice from trying to get through to him.

"He'll kill you, he'll kill Gabriela, he'll kill Greta, he'll kill Aurora, he'll kill Matteo." He cried out, "he'll kill us all, and he'll make us watch. That man is a monster-,"

"That wants to marry me! Don't let him take me, please, dad, please. Don't let him kill me."

He slid down the fridge, his knees seeming to give up under him as I laid helplessly on the island. The bottles of opened cheap beer all over the floor were broken, and the kitchen that was once filled with laughter and lively conversation, was now filled with the sound of a broken father weeping for the hopeless fate that his daughter would live.

I had just gotten out of the shower, and as I walked into the bedroom, I found Agostino standing around the bar in his room, pouring himself a glass of whiskey with ice. His back was to me, but he turned his head when I walked into the room, his eyes drinking in the sight of my naked body and wet hair clinging to my face. "there are two times you look the most beautiful in my eyes," he paused, turned his head and continued to pour his drink, "the first is when I've just fucked you and you're laying there, trying to catch your breath while calming down from your high," he turned with the glass in his hand, "and the second is when you just step out of the shower."

I hoped that he wouldn't see that I had been crying hours ago, but I had looked at myself in the mirror in the bathroom and the puffiness around my eyes had gone down and my eyes were no longer red. I almost looked like myself but I hoped that he wouldn't ask too many questions about it, so I would make conversation and not give him time to pay attention to me.

I didn't care to put on any clothes, there seemed to be no point of it because Agostino preferred it off. I walked over to the bed and sat on the edge of it, placing my legs beneath me as I looked up at him. " well, how was the rest of your day?" I asked him, tilting my head a bit to the side.

He walked over to me, taking a gulp of his drink. "nothing too important happened," he told me as he wrapped his hand around the back of my neck, playing with my wet hair. He leaned down and pressed his lips to mine before he began to move them in slow motions, kissing me in a way that made my toes curl and my breath come out short and quick. If there was one thing that I would give to Agostino was that he was a man of action- the way he did things- he did them well. From sex, to well, killing.

He detached his lips from mine and began to kiss down my neck. I craned my neck, my eyes closed as I let out soft sighs at the action, feeling his teeth bite into my skin. I bit my bottom lip, my hands suddenly on his shoulders, the harder that he sucked on my skin. He pulled away when he had done so to his satisfaction, my body tingling from the simple action. He stood tall like he always did, "I want to see those lips wrapped around my cock, get to it." He demanded, his voice stern and dominant.

Like the submissive slave that I was to his desires, my hands made their way to his belt and undid it. "I wanted to ask you something," I began as I unzipped his pants. I looked up at him through my lashes, my hands seeming to know their way even though I didn't look since I had done this what has felt like a million times before. "about your cousin, the don."

Agostino furrowed his eyebrows, "you really need to work on what is appropriate to talk about at times like this," he told me as his hand made its way to the back of my head and gripped onto my hair. His cock stood semi hard before my face and I wrapped my hands around it, my pussy throbbing in excitement for what was to come.

How I could go from completely despising this man to suddenly wanting to be fucked by him until I lost sense of reality, was beyond me?

I ran my tongue along the tip of the head, licking the precum that escaped the tip of the head and tasting it. The grip on my hair tightened in a way that made me know that he liked what I was doing. I began to play about with the head of his cock, sliding my tongue around it, moving in soft motions as I made him harder for me. "well," I paused, feeling his member harden in my hands, rising to its full length, "you know, between you and I," I looked up at him, preparing to swallow his cock- which no matter how many times I had it in my mouth- was always a difficulty to fit the whole thing. "I'm sure he's great at, you know, running the family business," Agostino watched me with his usual grey eyes, not giving anything away, but I knew that he wanted me to get to sucking him as though it were my lifeline, "but...he's not you."

I was being honest, looking at the two, they seemed to be complete opposites. Quite frankly, I hate to say it, but Agostino is the one who seems better suited to be the kind of man who ran such a thing. Agostino seemed to have exactly what all the others lacked in his family, but the current don...wasn't exactly, in my opinion fit for such a thing. Agostino should be the one in that position, or he should be trying to get into that position.

Sounds of slurping and gagging filled the room as I felt the tip of Agostino's cock in the very back of my throat, cutting off my air supply, as I used my hands to cover the remainder of his length. My eyes got teary, drool all over my mouth as I happily moved him in and out of my mouth. Doing it the exact way that he had trained me to do. His grip was tighter than ever, and I kept my eyes on his dark ones, watching them get hooded and watching as his breaths got shorter and the way his eyes peered into my own that made me feel proud to have a man like him weak in my hands...and mouth.

"There is a certain way that things are done," he responded, his voice almost strained but still steady. "I was a lot younger all those years ago, and he was more suitable."

I pulled back, letting out breaths and trying to catch my breath, "don't you want to be the don?" I asked him, but before I could say anymore he shoved his cock back into my mouth.

A smirk spread across his face as he looked down at me, "it's a lot of responsibility."

"You were younger then," I gasped, trying to catch my breath yet again, "but you aren't anymore. You shouldn't be taking orders from anyone," he chuckled, but I was almost as surprised as he was at my questions even though they were true. He didn't seem like a man who took orders and is a follower.

"These things take time...and need patience," he lined his cock in my mouth and I stuck out my tongue as he placed it gently on it before sliding his cock in. "lots of patience," he told me as he tossed his glass behind him, shattering it on the wall as he grabbed the back of my head with both of his hands and began to thrust furiously into and out of my mouth. "but," my eyes shut, trying to keep up with the pace but it was impossible. "if there's one thing I can tell you," I felt his hips buck and felt his cock twitch as his movements became more rapid and urgent, "is that this year, will be my year."

CHAPTER 19

I was honestly sick and tired of being afraid and feeling dreadful. Was it so much to want to go a day without feeling anxious, without being afraid of looking into Agostino's eyes and him finally snap and take me to his basement? I wanted things to go back to the way that they were. I missed the simplicity of life before all of this luxury that came at a price.

I missed being back home, back home in South Africa, in my tiny flat that I shared with my mum and grandma. I wish that I had treasured those moments a whole lot more than I did at that time. I wish that in those moment, I would have realised how precious they were. And I wasn't talking about the big moments, it was the little moments- those moments when we would sit on the sofa that my mum bought that were still covered in plastic because my grandma refused to remove it to "protect the sofas from any damage".

I miss the days when it was 20:00 and we would rush to put on SABC 1 and watch Generations, or the days when my mum would suddenly play gospel music on a random Sunday and I would just know that it was time to start "spring cleaning".

I didn't really remember a lot about the big moments, but the little things...they were what kept me up at night and made me shed a tear, or those random moments when I'm sitting in the back of Rolls Royce, being escorted around Merton. I missed how we would struggle to fit in the bathroom all at once but we would still do it. We would have my grandma in the bathtub, shouting at me to pass her the Sunlight bar soap so that she could scrub her body, and my mum would be sitting on the toilet, her eyes still red from the obvious hangover as she peed and repeatedly hushed my grandmother and I, and I would be standing at the sink, brushing my teeth while making sure that I didn't leave the dye too long in my hair. I missed the moments when we would laugh at people and each other, the moments when we would accidently fall asleep on the couch, or argue about who ate whose left over chicken.

The little things.

I was feeling sick to my stomach, literally. I had vomited several times already and I was under the weather, and it only added to my misery. The stylists were concerned about me, even though I had gotten ready an hour ago and was ready for pictures, I could barely stand still. They had left the room and left me alone for some time while I had my hand on the wall beside the bathroom door, trying to catch my breath and relieve my nausea but it wasn't helping. "I hear that you're not feeling well," I almost jumped in surprise at the sudden intrusion of Agostino's voice.

I shut my eyes, grinding my teeth against each other because I honestly didn't want to see him at the moment. "don't you know that it's bad luck to see the bride before the wedding?" as though

I didn't already have bad luck as it is, and if I were to even stub my toe one more time, I was certainly going to end my life. My voice was raspy and tired, and you could hear that I wasn't well.

I didn't want to turn around and look at him because I knew that he would look good, as he always does, but I knew that today he would be even better and I didn't need that right now. I was already in my wedding dress, perhaps the most beautiful dress that I have put on in my life, and if it wasn't for Agostino, I knew that I wouldn't have been able to ever afford a dress like this.

The wedding dress was a ball gown, and it had the elements of a fairy tale wedding that I always dreamed to have one day in my life. It had a sweetheart neckline and a tight corset that shaped around my upper body and hugged every bit of skin to make me appear slim and beautiful, with its off the shoulder long sleeves that stretch like vine across my fingers. Then from my waist, the dress formed the ball gown shape, large and voluminous with lots of tulle and material that made the dress heavy to wear and difficult to walk in. The dress was white, however it was sequined in a way that it made it as though the dress had been sprinkled with fairy dust, and it sparkled under any lighting. The dress had an 18 foot train behind me, and I looked like a queen- there was no other way to see it.

My ginger hair was pulled into a high yet messy bun with lots of curls, some that framed my face and some that added volume to my hair, like vines of curls all over my head and my make up was the most simple it's ever been, in a way that highlighted my natural beauty. You could see the freckles on my nose and you could see the beauty mark just above the corner of my top lip.

I felt him place his hands on my face and make me look at him. His eyes scanned my features, "I've been vomiting the whole morning," I said to him, choosing to say that instead as I looked into his eyes and looked at his face. I was jealous. How was it that I had to have makeup to make me look beautiful but a man as cold and evil as Agostino seemed to get better with each day, getting more handsome than he was the last time? I have been living with the man and I know that all he uses is a 3-in-1 body wash and he has no skin routine while I spend the better half of my life trying to get myself to look beautiful. "I'm just nervous though," I added with a sigh and shrug.

"I doubt that," he responded as he placed a gentle kiss to my lips even though I had told him that I had been throwing up. I mean, I did brush my teeth and the makeup artist had touched up on my face as though nothing had ever happened- but he didn't know that.

"Why would you say that?" I asked him with a light scoff. Was he that oblivious to the fact that I was so miserable and didn't want to marry him? If so, he was either delusional, which we agree that he obviously is, or I was a great actress to have made him believe that I actually wanted to do this. I was hoping that I could just call off the wedding, and somehow manage to get him to agree to cancelling, but it was a far shot.

"Because I know that you're pregnant." He responded casually as he began to adjust the cuff links, while he looked at me from head to toe.

I let out what sounded like a part laugh, part scoff, part gasp sound, "what? No, I'm not." I said as though he were retarded, in which he was.

"You're three weeks along. I was beginning to get concerned because you weren't showing the obvious tell-tale signs of pregnancy, but apparently pregnancy is different for everyone. However, I thought that the doctor was lying because you weren't showing any signs of morning sickness, increased urination, backache, but you have been really tired and sleeping a lot, so I let him live. So-"

"What the fuck do you mean I'm pregnant?" I snapped, looking at him as though he had grown two heads, "I'm not pregnant. I'm feeling sick because I don't want to fucking go out there and do this," I gestured between the two of us.

"I guess the mood swings have started early," he only said, just looking at me as though he was expecting this but I shook my head and turned around, picking up as much of the dress as I could as I tried to walk away from him.

There was no way that I was pregnant, no way. I couldn't be pregnant...God, no, I can't be pregnant. I haven't been feeling sick and, I was only tired because I was so depressed about my situation. There was no such thing as me being pregnant. I would know if I was pregnant.

And how would you know that exactly?

"I'm not pregnant," I chose to say aloud, fighting any intrusive thoughts. Is that why Agostino wasn't allowing me to drink these past few weeks? "I'm not pregnant. I can't be pregnant."

"Sit down, my dove," he said as he walked towards me, "don't make yourself upset, it might harm the baby."

"Stop that," I said with a straight face as I looked at him deathly in the face, "stop saying that," I said with a straight tone, refusing to let him tell me this at a time as sensitive as right now.

"stop saying that I'm pregnant when I'm not," my voice slowly raised, and the back of my throat began to burn, "I'm not...I'm not." I said more sternly.

Now that I thought about it, my heart raced because I realised how true this might all be. We have been having unprotected sex since the very first day. Who knows, I might have been pregnant then too but lost the baby because of the whole feeding me glass incident? It wouldn't explain a lot since I wasn't expecting it, but I thought that I could somehow stop any chance of falling pregnant.

By what? Praying it away? He was cumming in you almost every day, Delaney. What did you expect?

I began to cry, because I realised that Agostino wouldn't lie to me. He may be delusional, but he was an honest psycho who always told it to me like it was. So if he was telling me that I was pregnant, then I was. And at this point it was obvious that I was. I'm surprised it didn't happen sooner but I was terrified because I had made myself believe that I wouldn't fall pregnant. I couldn't bear him a child while I was still a child.

I began to cry, unable to stop myself, "no," I shook my head, but I felt him wrap his arms around me and pull me into his chest.

This was why he wanted to marry me.

It had been what felt like several hours since Agostino revealed to me that I was pregnant with his child, and it made me feel numb to everything. I had cried when he had told me but now I found my mind blank and my emotions were too strong to simply focus on one; so I just became numb. I stood with my bouquet in my hands, and a veil atop my head covering me. I was supposed to walk down the aisle in seconds, so I just stood there, waiting for Alessandro.

"Delaney," I looked up at the sound of my name being called, and looked into the comforting eyes of Alessandro who seemed to be taking me in. "you look…" he stopped, swallowing. I looked at him and his attire. He was wearing an expensive looking tuxedo, and I knew that there was no way Alessandro could ever afford that, so it was definitely courtesy of Agostino.

"Alessandro-" I accidentally interrupted him.

"I've made my decision," he said instead, cutting me off and rendering me silent. I furrowed my brows and looked at him in confusion. "I can't let you go through with this. I know the kind of monster that this man is, and if that means," he took a step closer to me and gripped my hand in his, "sacrificing myself, then so be it."

My heart began to race in anticipation as I looked at him with wide and anxious eyes, "what do you mean?" I asked, looking around me to make sure that Agostino wasn't suddenly standing close by and would hear what my father said and kill him. I looked around for any of his loyal men that guarded the place and found three of them positioned about.

"There's a car waiting for you outside right now, that will take you out of here and to the airport, and when you get there, you get your ass on that plane and you leave for New Orleans. You need to listen to me," his grip only got tighter and my heart dropped to my stomach in fear for what my father was saying. I began to shake my head in disagreement, "listen to me, listen to me, you have to always keep moving, keep moving, never stay in one place. Hopefully by the end of this week, you can go back to South Africa, and hide a bit better because he doesn't have contacts there. Are you listening to me, Delaney?" there was panic and desperation in his voice but looking into his eyes, the fear was overwhelming in his orbs. I could tell that he was deathly afraid.

"But...the guards?" I found myself croaking out.

"When these doors open, I'm going to do something, and when I do it, it will cause havoc and mayhem...and that will be your queue to run as fast as you can and get in that car." He held my hand in both of his, nodding his head to make me stop shaking mine in disagreement. "I love you, Delaney." He told me and I felt the tears sting my eyes before they escaped me.

"I love you too, Alessandro." I knew that he was going to do something drastic.

"Promise me you'll run, you'll run as fast and as far as you can. Promise me."

I cried, but nodded my head, "I promise."

He leaned down and placed a gentle kiss to my forehead through my veil. He stood beside me, placing his arm around me, and we stood in front of the doors, waiting for them to be pulled open. When they did, on cue, the music began playing- a violinist performing a masterpiece of "here comes the bride".

I couldn't take in my surroundings, my eyes found those of the man whose child I was carrying, the man I was destined to be with. Well, maybe I wouldn't say that. His grey eyes were taking me in, and he stood at the end of the aisle with the officiant. He looked good, he always did. He wore a white tuxedo, his hair was loose and framed him beautifully. He looked like a dream, handsome and all sorts of the kind of man one could only imagine themselves to be with. If the man wasn't a monster.

I felt my father drop my arm, and I turned to look at him, waiting to see what it was that he was about to do. He reached behind his back and pulled out a gun, before he raised it and pointed it at Agostino, whose eyes immediately landed on the gun. My heart stilled in the middle of the moment and things seemed to move in slow motion. I watched as Agostino became alert and so did his mafia family, but they hadn't been expecting it, so even when they drew their guns- it was after my father had begun pulling the trigger, shooting Agostino in the chest.

I didn't wait to see what would happen next, I knew that I would never get the chance again, so I ran. I turned and I ran as fast as I could, tossing the bouquet over my shoulder, ripping the veil off my head, grabbing the large dress to let me run faster, and dropping my glass heels behind...making my way towards freedom with the sound of gunfire lying in my wake.

Chapter 20

If this is what winning felt like, I wasn't too sure I had experienced a true victory. It has been three weeks since the day that my father had sacrificed himself for me. I can almost always hear the sound of gunfire as I dashed for the door, trying to get as far away from Agostino as possible. I didn't dare to look back because I knew that if I did, I would stop. So I ran, ran towards the Ford Mustang in the driveway, threw myself into the car, and heard the tyres screech as we got away. The driver was a man who held a beer in his hand and a cigarette in the corner of his lips, his tank top seemed old and worn, as if he cared very little for his appearance. Next to him was another man, one with darker hair and a solemn expression with a shotgun in his hand as he looked behind the car, keeping his eye on the road.

We drove through the forest, rarely using the road and somehow found ourselves at the airport. All they gave me was a pair of jean shorts, a black crop top, my passport, and an envelope that had some money in it. I got to New Orleans and stayed on the down low, living in some downturn rundown restaurant with too many cockroaches, but I didn't dare complain. I was sick too, morning sickness, fatigue- all pregnancy symptoms. And then four days later I left the country and made my way back home.

Gabriela and the kids were safe, they had managed to leave Merton the night before the wedding- right after I had left- and they were hiding away, but we wouldn't keep in touch to make sure that Agostino wasn't trailing me.

Being back home...it was different. I found myself in Port Elisabeth, living in some elderly woman's backrooms made of zinc. I had to use a bucket as a toilet, and I didn't even have a bed, but I didn't care. I felt free, away from a man who could take my life at any given moment. I wanted to be back home, in my flat, but I knew that would be the first place that Agostino would look for me. However, he didn't have contacts in South Africa, so I was safe. This was my homeland. I knew this place like the back of my hand, I knew the people and I was fluent in the language. I was safe.

I wasn't stupid though, for a week I stayed still, and then finally, after three weeks I decided that it was time that I went through with my pregnancy termination. I knew that this baby was what was connecting me to Agostino, and he wasn't going to rest until he had his child. So I had to do it. I had to get rid of this baby before I got attached. I was a kid too, dammit, I was only 20 years old, and even though my birthday was in a month- I felt like I was still 13. I wasn't in space to be a mother, and I wasn't going to go through nine months of carrying a child that I wouldn't be able to give my all to.

Agostino had taken a lot from me. He had raped me, taken advantaged of me and enslaved me. Not to mention, my father had to die in order to get me out of that situation. There was no other way around it, I couldn't bring a piece of Agostino into this world. What needed to happen, was for the world to go without an Agostino. I believed that he was dead, I prayed day and night that God had taken his life and took him to Hell. The shot my father delivered was a deadly one, and I hoped that it pierced his heart.

I looked over my shoulder, looking at all of the different faces of women who were walking into the abortion clinic with me. All their faces like mine; their complexions different shades of brown, some were laughing, others quiet, but everyone minded their own business. I shuffled on my feet, accidently dropping a R20 (Rand) and bending down to pick it up before I kept moving with the crowd. The clinic was a cheap building, a lot of things were like that in our country, but unlike before, I revelled in it now. I wanted to cry just sitting on the cheap plastic chairs, hearing nurses scold patients, and hearing several cries of babies whose restless mothers tried to calm. It felt good to be in a familiar environment again.

I was wearing an old maxi dress that I had bought from a fat woman who was sitting on a crate under the blistering hot sun, selling second hand clothing on the side of the road. The dress was a light yellow and it was kind of pretty. My hair was in a ponytail, and I nervously wrung my fingers, trying hard to not think too hard about what I was about to do.

I was very much so prochoice, and I believed that we were allowed to make whatever decision we wanted to as women. However, that didn't mean that the decision wasn't difficult. A part of me tried to convince me to keep the child, but I knew that the right thing to do was get rid of it and bury all remnants of my past life. I had to move on and forget.

I looked at the girl next to me. She looked much too young to be in a place like this. Her face was small and childlike and she looked like she couldn't be older than 15 years old, and she sat holding hands with an old woman who was obviously her grandmother. I looked over her face, a part of me wondering what it could be that made her end up in a place like this with the small round stomach that she tried to hide. Was it rape? I wouldn't be surprised, South Africa is the rape capital of the world and stories like this were all too common. Maybe she had a boyfriend, a boy that she liked and they got carried away and now she's here? Again, all too common.

I was lost in thought, lost in this girl with a small afro and round lips. Her eyes teary and afraid and her grandmother pacifying her and telling her that it was okay, so they made conversation with each other. In a way, the warmth and gentleness of the grandmother's voice reminded me so much of my own grandmother who would take care of me and cater for me in the gentlest way possible. A small smile spread across my face at the memory of my grandmother before my body sensed someone taking a seat next to me.

The whiff of expensive Italian cologne hit me like a ton of bricks and ripped the smile off my face as I froze.

I looked down at my feet, noticing the shiny black Italian leather shoes next to mine that were in simple brown sandals. I swallowed, my eyesight becoming blurry and the back of my throat burning as my heart began to pound. "this is no place for a lady," I heard the voice say. A voice I would never forget, the voice of the don. He let out a sigh, leaning back in the cheap plastic chair as I sat silent, looking ahead, and felt a tear escape my eye.

There it was, the emotion that I had thought that I had escaped. Fear.

I was overwhelmed by it and it washed over me in a way that only they could make me feel. My heart dropped to my stomach and it felt like someone had forced a bag of desert sand into mouth because it suddenly ran dry. I couldn't say anything, couldn't get any words to form because I knew that they had found me and they were going to take me back. I gripped onto the material of the cheap and flimsy dress, my hands trembling. "I understand, well, at least, I try to understand." He began, crossing his legs, speaking in a calm tone, "it's a lot like when you keep your chickens in a coop, and you lock them up in there, day and night, only expecting them to lay eggs, only opening the door once in a while- it creates this sense of wonder, this desire to break free and go out there. It's okay to wan to run free, even if it's for a little moment," he paused, and I sensed him turn his head towards me. "but it's time for the Autumn dove to return to her nest." He placed a hand on my trembling ones, "come on."

He wasn't giving me a choice.

I finally found my voice, "I'm not going back there," I croaked out, my voice trembling and afraid. My eyes still looking ahead, hoping that one of the nurses would sense the danger that I was in and help me but what could they even do? He would kill them, he was the don, and he would probably get away with it too.

"We have them. All of them." I knew who he was talking about before he even said their names. They had Gabriela and the children.

I couldn't help the cry that escaped me as I buried my face in my hand, because the chances were that I was returning for my death. "he's going to kill me." I said in a fearful tone, trying to calm my racing heart but I knew that I had no choice.

"He wants you home. Tonight."

CHAPTER 21

The word terrified doesn't even begin to describe what I was feeling at the moment. The past 19 hours have been horrendous, sitting in close proximity to the very man that was the relative of a man that I hoped was dead- it was gut wrenching. The don was calm and casual, as if he had done this one too many times. And finally, here I was, back in that damned town, the Cadillac Escalade parked in the driveway of the dreaded modern mansion that belonged to Agostino.

"I have to say, Autumn dove, I didn't think that someday this would be you." The don finally said, breaking the silence and managing to speak over my pounding heart and short and panicked breaths.

I couldn't stop the flow of tears, or the way that my body was trembling. I knew that once I stepped out of this car and into that home, horrors only awaited me. I knew that the don was Agostino's cousin but at this point, I just needed someone to listen to me. I just needed to talk, even if it was to an enemy, "I don't want this life," I said in between quivering and weak cries. I let out a saddened breath, watching as the door was opened for me by one of the men outside. I turned my head and looked at the don, "I'll die running from him." I bravely said, before I turned my head and accepted the hand that the man was offering.

I let him help me out of the car before he led me into the home. Each step, it felt as though my feet were being cemented into the ground and it got harder to move forward. If it wasn't for Gabriela and the kids, I probably wouldn't have come all this way. But then again, I realise that Agostino is a man that has no heart and he was going to kill them either way so I shouldn't have made the effort to come back because it won't change anything.

The home looked as spotless as it always does, the servants walked around the house, brushing off invisible dust and making sure that the home barely had any space left for a microsome of dirt. I didn't look at any of them, kind of feeling judged by their wordless behaviour, as if they scoffed at me and my attempt of getting away...again. I wondered if some saw me as brave or if they all just saw me as stupid. I had a feeling it was the latter.

I tried to think of other things, trying to put myself in a more positive mindset preparing for what was about to come but my impending doom was all that I could think about. The man led me to the very spot where Agostino and I had our first date, the night where we sat and dined over his stingrays, overlooking the town of Merton. The sun had set long ago and goosebumps broke out over my arms, and the hairs on the back of my neck rose. It felt too much like the very day that he and I had begun. Except this time, I wasn't naïve, I knew exactly what he was capable of and I knew that no good could come of this.

He stood, with his hand in his pocket, and the other holding a glass of whiskey. He stood as though he were a king overlooking his kingdom. He wore a black pants, and he was shirtless. The wind blowing through his curly hair that wasn't as done as it usually is. My feet were rooted to the ground, not wanting to get too close to him because I didn't want to get hurt.

We stood in silence for what felt like forever, my body shivering from the cold and fear. "I've been thinking of ways to hurt you," he finally said, his voice coming out calm and collected, but the words being carried by the winds to my ears. "I give you everything, and you turn and run."

I dug my nails into my palms, trying to catch my breath, "I wasn't happy. I was afraid," I began, slowly raising my voice and being surprised that I was talking, "afraid of you, afraid of your love- afraid of everything. That's not okay." I said with tears, crying and hoping that my words would somehow make sense to his delusional mind.

He turned and I evaded his eyes, "I'm going to hurt you, so bad...so bad, that you will never be okay again." he told me, walking towards me while I took an unsteady step back, my eye sight blurry and my heart racing with more vigour.

"Why are you doing this to me?" I cried, my gut wrenching, "why are you hurting me?" the torture had not even begun but I was already a mess. "I will never stop, Agostino, I will never stop trying to get away from you! I will keep running!" I gasped, yelling at the top of my lungs and glaring at his blank face that gave nothing away and those grey eyes that were unforgiving and glaring into my own as though he had all the time in the world. I wanted to hurt him, "this...thing inside me, I'll kill it! I swear to God I'll kill it!"

The glass of whiskey in his hand suddenly shattered under his tight grip, the shards of glass stabbing into his hand but he didn't say anything. "I'll cut your legs from right under you and you will never walk again. If you ever leave me, it will be with you crawling on your stomach, digging into the ground with bloody fingers; only for me to come up and drag you back with me." he was standing in front of me, his hand gripping my face and forcing me to keep looking at him, "the only way you'll ever leave me, is in a fucking wooden box while I make sure I bury you twelve feet under."

He began to drag me, and I began to fight; screaming, kicking and crying. He dragged me all the way to the elevator and down to his basement. I bit him wherever I could, pulling his hair, dug my nails into his skin, tried to claw his eyes out but he was able to escape each of my attacks. He dragged me down the dreaded basement that I still had nightmares about and when that secret door opened and showed me into the basement, I stood in shock for only a split second before I let out several uncontrollable wails and sobs at the sight that met me.

Alessandro's body dangled from a brown rope that was tied around his neck, his face black and rotted with flies all around it. His stomach had been sliced open, his guts on the floor and the lion in the corner seemed to be enjoying his intestines. Gabriela and Greta were also dangling from brown ropes, except they were standing on stools that with a gentle and swift kick, would end up with them getting hung. They both had their hands tied behind their backs and their faces were bright with tears, the smell of urine strong in the air, and I could see that both of them had thrown up over themselves.

"If you look away, even for a second, I will have the cook turn on the oven and put 6 year old Matteo in there and leave him to cook. And if you try to stop me, I will have Aurora swimming with the stingrays, do you understand?" Agostino said but I began to plead with him.

"Agostino please, please!" I cried, standing still because there was no way that I could do anything or else things were only going to get worse for Matteo and Aurora and I couldn't have anything happen to them. I watched as Agostino pulled out a saw.

"They call this the camping saw, it ideally cuts small branches for firewood," he paused, turning around and looking at me, "today, I'll be gauging out eyes with it. The fun thing is that you get to decide who I do it to, so," he walked towards Greta and Gabriela who began crying and pleading with him. "who loses their eyes?"

I fell to my knees and begged him, "please, please, Agostino."

"Are you trying to stop me?" he said in a deathly tone, reminding me that if I ever tried to, then Aurora would pay the price.

I hurriedly shook my head, "no, no."

"I don't have patience to wait for you to make your decision. I will take out the eyes of this little girl."

"No!" I said, before I sobbed, looking between the two of them and realised that I would sadly have to make Gabriela go through it instead of her daughter. "Gabriela...do," I sobbed, "do it to Gabriela."

I wanted to shut my eyes and look away but Matteo's life was on the line and I knew that Agostino would put him in the oven. I watched as Agostino walked towards Gabriela and gripped her face, forcing her face to be still as she cried and begged, screaming as she watched him bring the saw closer to her eyes. We all let out collective screeches of horror as Agostino brutally drove the saw into Gabriela's eye balls, digging out her eye as blood gushed out everywhere. Gabriela's legs kicked in ferocious pain and her blood curdling screams would haunt me forever, as Agostino walked towards me and placed her completely destroyed eyeball in my hand before he walked back and gauged out the other.

I wanted to look away from the gory sight but I couldn't. Greta was a blubbering mess, peeing on herself and vomiting all at once. I was no better because I could barely keep anything in my stomach and Agostino told me that if I dared drop the eye, then he would make sure he would replace it with Greta's.

He walked back to me, his face and chest covered in Gabriela's blood. I wailed uncontrollably, in a way that was inhumane and horrified as I heard the lion raw in the far corner of the room, probably irritated with us and our loud cries, but then again, it might be used to it. "be a doll and give that to the lion," he gestured towards the eyes and the rest of Alessandro's insides. "I'll be back tomorrow morning to take someone's fingers and toes, so make an executive decision."

I hate to do this, but I'm currently in final year and it's exam season/assigment season at this time of the semester so I'm really focusing a lot on school- with trying to maintain my distinctions (your girl's smart like that) so I'm gonna have to go on a bit of a hiatus for a couple of weeks. Maybe two or three, and then I'll be back with more.

Toodles!

CHAPTER 22

The thing with life is that each of our journeys are different; some individuals journeys follow the typical fairy tale route- they grow up in a perfect home, a loving parent or both loving parents, they grow in a supportive community, and in that environment of love, they flourish and end up loving someone and therefore repeating the process. Other individuals aren't as lucky, others grow up without any parents, others grow up in an environment filled with hate and despair and so on and so forth. Maybe I'm just naïve in this viewpoint as I was all those months ago when I set my eyes on the devil...however, never in my wildest nightmares did I ever think that I would be as unfortunate as I am right now at this thing called life.

Life had done more than just disappoint me...it had wholeheartedly and unbelievably so, fucked me up.

Agostino had officially broken me without ever laying a hand on me. I was completely destroyed; mentally, emotionally, and physically. I stood, silent, my heart beating at the slowest pace that it ever has as I looked at the two closed caskets being lowered into the ground. Matteo clung onto my leg, hopelessly wailing, and Aurora fell to the ground, crying uncontrollably as her mother and father were lowered into the ground. Greta on the other hand, she was as blank as I was, as emotionless and distant as I was at the moment, and the memories of moments leading to this right here flashed through my mind.

We had spent three days in here, and Gabriela was being tortured. Agostino purposely didn't gag her so that we would be forced to hear her cries and wails of agony. He had pulled out her fingers and toes, then the next day he cut off her ears, to the point where I began begging him to put her out of her misery. Even she began to plead and cry, her mouth gurgling as he sliced off her tongue because he didn't want to hear her voice.

The secret door opened and light entered the dark room, the lion in the corner just sat there, watching us but I was so used to it by now. I laid hopelessly on the floor that was covered in Gabriela's blood, and I just looked at the two people who were paying for my sins. Greta's face had turned purple, and Gabriela looked like a ghost, she had lost a lot of blood and she looked like something straight out of a horror movie, yet she still cried and gurgled out blood every few moments from pain.

Agostino walked through the door, holding Matteo and Aurora with one of each hand and the door closed behind them. I rushed to my feet, watching as Matteo and Aurora screamed in horror at the sight of their mother and what she had obviously been through. They cried and cried, and I cried with them and so did Greta. The room was filled with shattered sobs of traumatised children and I couldn't imagine how difficult this was for them. Their father's carcass hung from the ceiling, surrounded by flies and insects, their mother was a gory sight for their innocent eyes, and their sister was dangling from the ceiling, turned purple and covered in vomit and urine and stool.

"It's time to end this," Agostino said to me as I looked into his blank and emotionless eyes. He didn't care, and he wasn't moved by the sobs of the children and it was in that moment that I realised what a real monster this man was, and I was going to be forced to give him his child. "put her out of her misery, Delaney. Kick the chair and hang her." He told me blankly, his words commanding and unforgiving.

I began to cry, shaking my head because I didn't want to do that to her. I couldn't kill her, but looking at her now, there was no point. She had to, she had to rest and the only way she was going to rest was if she died. However, I didn't have it in me to kill her.

"If you don't," Agostino paused, "I'll feed Matteo to the lion." He grabbed Matteo and began to walk towards the lion that stood to attention at the meal making its way towards it.

I ran towards Agostino, grabbing the lower part of Matteo with all intention of pulling him away from Agostino. "no! no!" I cried while Aurora and Greta uncontrollably called for their brother. "okay, okay I'll do it! Don't hurt him, please!" my voice was completely shattered.

Agostino walked back towards me and I walked over to Gabriela. "I'm so sorry for putting you through this, Gabriela," I apologised for the millionth time. Hoping that she would find it in her heart to forgive me for all of this. Never in my wildest nightmares did I think that this would happen to her, or anyone. I didn't think people like Agostino existed but now, now I understood why they called him dono della morte, "the gift of death". Because when it came to Agostino, him granting you death, was truly the greatest mercy. "I'm sorry, Gabriela," I cried as I lifted my leg and kicked the stool; causing her to dangle from the ceiling by the brown rope around her neck. Her legs kicked from underneath her, and I could hear her struggling and the sound of death was painful and would haunt me forever. She gagged, unable to say anything, her legs kicking, her body fighting- then suddenly-... it fell silent.

Aurora let out a shrill scream at the sudden stillness of her mother, and it will forever echo in my mind the way her scream sounded of horror and heartbreak.

And then Agostino whispered to me, smug and cold, in what would be the weakest moment of my entire existence, "I told you I'd break you..."

The entire town was here- witnessing the funeral. No one said anything but I knew that this wasn't a first for them. They had probably witnessed plenty funerals caused by Agostino, and they had been probably counting down the days that I would be as unfortunate as his previous women. I couldn't look any of them in their faces- not like they even dared to look at any place other than my feet whenever I came across anyone.

Their caskets were fancy and expensive, and everything about the service had been top tier. However, no amount of fancy could cover up the fact that they had died at the merciless torture of Agostino. If anything, it felt like a further spat in the face that he could bring them so much misery and then simply cover it up with his wealth and a shiny brown box.

We stood there until the sun had set and people had walked away, except for Gabriela's older sister who tried to comfort

Aurora who was still uncontrollably crying. I held Matteo as tightly as I could, wrapping my arms around him in a way that would show him how sorry I was. I knew that they would grow up to hate me, I could sense that Greta would never forgive me for putting her parents through this; and quite honestly, I hate myself too. I won't be okay and I probably will never be.

"You take good care of them," I said to Gabriela's sister, Elena who was a middle aged single woman who seemed to be enjoying her life until I called her a few days ago and told her about what had happened. I didn't tell her that Agostino had killed her sister, just that they had met up in an accident and died, and for her to come to Merton and take the kids to take care of them wherever her heart desires.

She gave me a small heartbroken smile as she gave me a half hug, "I will. I'll try my best." I hoped that she would take them as far away from Merton as possible and try to give them a better life that would at least suppress the memories of their mother's torture and their fathers butchered body. Agostino had given her a fat suitcase of money and told her that he would create three trust funds for the kids to be able to pursue their passions and so on and so forth.

I stood there, watching as they walked to the car that the sister had rented. I watched my half siblings walk away from me, watching their fallen shoulders and dreaded walks towards a life without a mother or father.

That's when I cried.

I placed my hand over my mouth, crying because Agostino was right. He had broken me... he had taken everything away from me and all that I had left at this point, was him. That seemed to be a fate far worse than death. Not only had he taken everything away from me, but he had taken everything away from all the people that I had cared about; he had taken life from my father and Gabriela and he had taken everything away from my siblings. Him letting me live with the guilt of all my decisions would surely drag me into a self-created hell.

I watched as they got into the blue Volvo and drove away, getting further and further away from me. I knew Agostino was watching me, but he made himself known and the need to go home after the blue Volvo had disappeared out of sight. "let's go." He told me as he wrapped his arm around my waist and made me walk beside him, making our way to the convoy of BMW's. I climbed into he BMW X7 and stared out of the window, watching as we drove away from the cemetery, my eyes looking at the two freshly dug graves before I looked away and ahead.

CHAPTER 23

Hello, my child

This is my seventh journal entry, and I found myself looking forward to it the whole of last night as I laid beside your father. It's also yet another day that I haven't said a word to your father, or even myself. I'm starting to believe that I have forgotten what my voice even sounds like. I don't recognise myself in the mirror anymore, my eyes don't shine at all; instead they look dead and void of anything lively. I have stopped crying myself to sleep, so that's the upside.

Your dad is concerned- mostly about you because the doctor said it's not good that I have fallen into a deep depression.

To be honest, I have only begun to realise how deep, dark, gruelling and painful depression truly is. I thought me being on the brink of killing myself two years ago was true depression, but this, this right here is so much worse. I can't escape it, I can't run from it- a lot like how I can't escape and run from your father. All I feel is emptiness, an emptiness that doesn't allow me to enjoy the beauty of the world around me or even be present in my conscience.

I feel you kicking and playing around in my stomach most times- your father loves it- and while it is quite beautiful and exciting, I wish you didn't kick my ribs half as much as you do. You're quite the healthy baby, and the doctor says you're going to be a baby boy. I couldn't even smile when I heard the news because I suddenly realised that there was a possibility that you were going to end up like your father; a monster who might repeat this cycle that your father has created.

A baby boy is all that he had been wanting- someone to take over his empire that he's planning on building.

I cried...as though it was the day of the funeral all over again.

I'm sorry son. I love you so very much, however the version of you that you could possibly become is the part of you that I will hate.

I don't think I'll ever let you read this journal, I'll probably throw it into the fire and watch it burn with all of my thoughts and deepest worries. There's no doubt your father probably knows exactly what I write here, but at this point I don't care. I just want to get some things off my chest, even though it's only through a fine ballpoint pen and not through my lips.

I hope I can get over this and I hope that I don't live the rest of my life as sad and miserable as I am right now. I just want to be happy again...but I feel like I'm already asking for too much. Maybe I don't deserve happiness, but maybe I deserve peace. Peace with the way that my life has turned out. I have gotten over the first obstacle; acceptance. I have accepted that this is my life and I will never leave, hell, probably not even through death. Your father has claimed me, made me his property and the recipient of his twisted love that he is so blind to its toxins. I can tell at times that he is confused about what's going on and why I am the way that I am.

I guess he was right, he did break me, but it seems like...he doesn't know that he did? I don't think he realises how badly he fucked me up, because to him, he didn't even try to hurt me, he simply brushed upon the surface. That's how sick of a man he is. However, even the most vile of men have a soft spot and I know that is you. I find him looking at your ultrasound pictures, his eyes so taken in with your tiny innocent body swimming in my bodily fluids.

I guess I have those moments too- when I look at your pictures and I wonder what you'll look like. I wonder about the size of your fingers, the way that your eyes will look, how you will look at me, the way your tiny mouth will form into a smile every time you look at me, or how your laugh may sound. My baby boy...

I pray, pray so hard that you never lose your innocence, that you never lose the very thing that will make you my child. However I am afraid that your future is already written and there is no way that you can escape your fate of turning into your father; turning into a monster who will rip the world apart and cause more harm than good. Your innocence will be short lived, but I'll try to capture every moment, and try to instill some humanity in you, even if it's just a tiny bit.

I closed the journal, placing the pen in between the pages before I sighed and placed the black leather bound book on the bed. I brushed a strand of hair behind my ear, and leaned against the pillows, my left hand absentmindedly rubbing my swollen belly as I looked across the room at the wall blankly.

There was a large TV that Agostino had installed that was currently running and playing my current TV show obsession: The Flash. It was the only thing that actually captured my attention and the only thing that I actually watched and enjoyed. The love story between Barry Allen and Iris West was enough to soften my broken heart and I marvelled at the fictional love story between the pair, the way that Barry would absolutely crumble at the mere sight of Iris' tears, and how he went against formidable enemies to protect her. Why couldn't I have that? Was I not deserving of a love like so? Instead, I was stuck with a man who loved me in a way that didn't allow me to be safe.

The door of the bedroom opened but I didn't let my eyes stray from the TV screen as I watched, captivated by a series that prior to right now, I probably wouldn't have spared any of my time on. However, I knew that it was Agostino, the way that the hairs on the back of my neck and my arms stood on end, and there was a sudden shift in the air as though even the natural elements were well aware of the dark man walking into the room. I heard some shuffling but didn't care to give him any of attention until I felt the bed dip next to me and I felt his large and gentle hand on my tummy, and the other gently caressing my face, brushing my hair out of my face, "my dear...my love...my Autumn dove," he recited in a gentle tone as though he wasn't the very bane of my existence.

It almost made me cry; how gentle he was at this moment, as though that broad chest of his actually contained a heart. His hands that only brought death and destruction to others were as gentle as they had been all those times when I had been unsuspecting of him; they actually felt loving. He touched me in a way as if he were afraid of breaking me.

He leaned forward and pressed a gentle kiss to my lips before he pressed his nose against mine and peered into my eyes. I couldn't break free from the eye contact because he shielded my entire view. His eyes gazed into my own, searching for me. He did this every day; he would come in, caress me and just peer into my eyes, calling for me, and I would just sit there. "come back to me," he called softly, his sultry voice sounding a lot like the man that I had fallen for. "how many more lives must I end until you respond to me?" he asked, and I blinked, thinking of those times that he had killed my therapists because they weren't able to bring me out of this depression.

I felt a tear escape me because yet again, I was the reason that other people died. "stop looking at me," I croaked out in a broken whisper that sounded nothing like me, but instead like a broken record that played in the distant corners of an abandoned warehouse.

At my words his grip tightened around the back of my neck, squeezing as though that was all that he had been searching for. "please...stop looking at me." I begged him, the scorching hot tears falling gracefully down my now fattened cheeks due to my pregnancy. "how do you expect me to carry on like everything is fine? Agostino, you did this to me. You broke me, every little bit of me, you took in your hands and you crushed it. I'm in the dark, I'm so lost in the dark and I just want to come out but I don't know how."

"La mia colomba autunnale," he said, his fingers gently massaging into my skin, the baby kicking in my belly at the caress of his father's hand on my belly, "I will never apologise because I don't regret a thing that I have done. You might not see it this way, but when it comes to you, you have made me soft. Because of you...three other people that I could have killed, live. Because of you...I was merciful towards your father and his wife. You might not see it...but I could have and would have done so much worse to you if you were not the one who held my heart."

I looked at him as though he were a monster, his words scaring me in a way far worse than I thought he was capable. He didn't sound like a man who felt apologetic for the things he had done, instead he sat here, telling me that he had gone easy on me?

"I fell in love with you the very moment that I laid my eyes on you. It's funny because there was a time in my life, many years ago, when I was still a little boy living under my father's wings, toothless and innocent- and, and he said to me that love would someday find me. And it was strange hearing these words from my father who was a hardened criminal, a man who was feared by almost everyone in the underworld, a man who could bring down the world's most powerful man- a man who would crumble at the mere sight of a smile from my mother. It was fascinating, but he held my tiny hand in his larger one that was covered in blood, and said that someday I would be as hardened as I need to be, but someone, a woman...or a man- he was open minded like that- would come into my life and take my frozen heart and melt it in a way that will change me. I believed him, but it got a little less every year that went by...until I didn't believe him at all.

That, was the day that I met you, standing behind the counter at the restaurant- your eyes wide and wandering, until they landed on mine. In that moment," his voice fell into a sultry whisper, his eyes never once breaking from mine, "I knew that I had found the one for me, and I would never let you go. I will never let you go. Most importantly," he paused, letting out a breath as he kissed my wet lips with salty tears, "I have forgiven you for trying to leave me. I don't expect your forgiveness, I don't need it. In my softness towards you, I have given you all of this time to deal with the loss and the grief, but I wont let you endanger my child anymore. You will get out of this bed and you will accept all of the help that I get for you, or else I might not be as gentle in my punishing you as I was the last time."

His words were cold and chilling, and I just looked at him with hate. Despising every bit of his being at the moment but he didn't care, if anything he was just blank and emotionless as he usually is.

"Good," he let go of the back of my neck and his hand trailed down to my left hand where he held it up, looking at the engagement ring that he had somehow recovered and placed back on my finger a day after the funeral. "we are going to get married in two days," he told me as though he was telling me about the sunny weather outside, "you ruined our previous one, but I doubt you'll ruin this one. However, there is something...very minor, that I am here to ask of you to do on our wedding...trust me," he paused, a dark smirk coming on his face, "it will change the course of our lives forever."

CHAPTER 24

Agostino said that me turning away at the aisle and running away had cursed our marriage, and we would be unfortunate if we didn't right our wrongs. So what was one way of doing that? Redoing our wedding in a way that his family traditions dictated to right a wrong; and that was how? By having me wear a black wedding dress and a black wedding veil that didn't even allow me to see anything. It was to show that I was regretful of the bad that I had done to my husband, and that I was apologetic, and from now onwards, the only person who would guide me through life would be Agostino.

Quite the fucking family tradition if you ask me.

I preferred to think of it as me treating this wedding as a funeral for all that I have ever known. This was a sad occasion for me, an occasion that I knew signalled the rest of my life that would now be dedicated to a man who had killed the only people I had left in the world. The black wedding dress was simpler than my previous wedding dress, but not in the least bit less beautiful. It wasn't a ball gown, but it graciously fell over my body like water, hugging my belly and bringing a certain kind of elegance to my pregnancy that I don't think that I have ever seen before. It was a matte satin, off the shoulder dress, with beaded tulle that formed a cape behind me. The sweetheart neckline that it created showed off my swollen breasts and my arms were covered in soft lace detail that seemed like vines created around my arms.

I looked at myself in the mirror, so taken aback by the difference from the last time that I stood here on my first wedding day. I felt like I had been younger then, as though unaware of the true danger that I was in. And today I stood here, fully pregnant, with no one by my side.

My hair was made into a low yet messy bun that created a look of graceful charm, making me look almost as youthful as I did back then. I heard a knock on the door but before I even responded, the handle turned and in walked Agostino's cousin- the don. My heart raced as I met his eyes through the mirror and he stood there for a second taking me in.

I turned around and smiled at him, dipping my head low in greeting and respect as he entered the room and one of his men closed the door behind him. "you look...different," he told me as he put his hands in the pockets of the expensive suit that he wore. I hated to say it, but the don was the one person that I actually cared to enjoy his company because I knew that he didn't need to answer to anyone, and he gave off the kind of energy of the uncle in your family that drank too much and would tell you outrageous stories that you knew were absolutely a lie.

He has been visiting me every once in a while, and when he does, he always manages to make me laugh and smile. I smiled, "yeah, I'm rounder than I was the last time you saw me." he approached me and placed his hand on my arm before he leaned in and placed two kisses on each of my cheeks.

"You carry pregnancy well, look at yourself in the mirror. You're the most beautiful you have ever been," he said with a smile like that of a father looking at his daughter and my throat tightened- and I had to break eye contact. "I was talking about the dress, black lady. My, I don't remember the last time anyone in my family witnessed a black wedding. In more ways than one," he uncontrollably chuckled at the terrible joke and I rolled my eyes but found myself laughing a little.

"Thank you for...coming to see me, and well...you know, everything." I said with a tight lipped smile, clearing my throat so that I wouldn't cry as I looked at the don and he smiled at me, nodding his head and shaking his hand in a dismissive manner as though it were no problem.

"Of course, walking you down the aisle is no big deal," he shrugged, and I looked down at my feet for a moment. He fell silent before he spoke up, "what's wrong with you?" he asked me as though he picked up that there was something wrong. I mean, he surely couldn't have gotten this far in the business if he wasn't able to pick up how someone was feeling or probably even thinking.

I looked up at him, just about to answer the question when the door to the bedroom opened and in walked Agostino followed by two of his other cousins that I dared not stand in the room when they were present because they gave off the kind of off putting energy like he did. There was Paolo who was the youngest at 27 years old and he was based in Italy, running things alongside the don but having to answer for every move that he makes and he clearly didn't like that. Then there was Giacomo who was 32 years old and he was based in New York City and he was far worse than Agostino, I have to say. He killed for any and every reason and he loved to get his hands dirty in blood.

I have come to learn that they were the three Amigos. The closest. They thought the same, acted the same and all wanted the same thing; to rule the Milano family mafia without Luigi.

Luigi stood facing me for a moment, his eyes going over my face, as if he knew that the three men were behind him but he was gathering info from my face. I nervously swallowed but finally looked away from the three men and then at Luigi, my eyes apologetic but his eyes holding the kind of venom and wisdom that a man who has been in this line of business for this long would possess.

He let out a scoff, his head moving back a bit before he placed both of his hands in his pockets and then turned around casually looking at the three men. "my boys," he greeted with a smile as Agostino approached us, while Paolo leaned against the door, swirling around a toothpick in his mouth. Paolo stood at 6 feet, and he had a bald head that was covered in tattoos. His eyes were hazel and he had droopy eyes that were always red as if he was always high.

Agostino told me that his eyes were always red because Paolo's mother had been a raging alcoholic and drug addict while she was pregnant with him, so Paolo happened to be a little stranger than usual. He was the assassin of the three of them. He never missed a shot. He always killed precisely and was never really a fan of torture but loved to have his men rape other men who had betrayed him. He would have his men capture the traitor, strip him of his clothing, and then have his men rape the captor while he would sit there, smoke, eat and laugh as though he could never get enough of it.

Giacomo stood at 6'3 and he loved himself an expensive trench coat and fedora that he used to conceal his eyes. I have only seen his face once, when I accidentally walked in on a meeting that he was having with Agostino. He had dark hair that was always neat and combed back, dark and thick eyebrows and a crooked nose as though he had broken it and didn't care to put it back into place. He had a neat beard, and while he did enjoy killing, he was more of a numbers guy. Agostino refers to him as "the accountant".

They had been planning this day for some time. Of course, I was unaware until two days ago when Agostino told me that it was time that things needed to be done the right way. He was going to have Paolo kill Luigi, and have Paolo take the fall for betraying the Milano family and have a bounty placed on his head.

Paolo sacrificing himself and killing Luigi would ensure that he would have no chance of being the don, thereby leaving Giacomo and Agostino. Giacomo has no interest in being the boss and prefers the role of the underboss who is in charge of the US and Mexico. Thereby leaving Agostino who will take this moment to rise to the occasion and take over Luigi's seat because Luigi has more than once claimed to have him take over the Milano family. Once Agostino is situated as the don, he'll remove the bounty off Paolo's head and make Paolo his left hand man aka the Consigliere.

I asked Agostino one simple question; why now? Why not all those months ago? Or in a year's time? His response was simple- I'm due in two months and he wants to get me to Italy so that I can get situated and give birth to a pure Italian son. Which means that we are leaving Merton behind and he will leave it to some other rookie to take over.

We are destined for greater things. We are destined to rule things- from Italy- take over Italy and the underworld...or so he says.

My duty was to get Luigi alone in my room. I was his favourite, Agostino said, so he would come if I were the one who called him.

"Tino," Luigi looked at the man who walked past him and towards me instead. Agostino wrapped his arm around me, bringing me to his body and placing a kiss on my forehead. Agostino wore a crisp black velvet suit that looked like it couldn't afford to get any blood on it.

"Luigi."

"I have been in this business a long time. 30 years, 30 years I have run this Milano family," Luigi spoke in Italian, that I happened to be fluent in at this point. He spoke with calmness and confidence as if he knew what they were trying to do but he wasn't all too bothered. He let out a chuckle, "I made you, each of you are who you are because of me. You never turn your back on family, do you, Tino?"

"Things always have to come to an end." Agostino responded blandly, lacking emotion- even empathy- towards a man who was like a father to him. I realised then, and a long time ago, that to Agostino the only thing that mattered was power.

The room fell silent and sombre for a moment. I didn't make eye contact with Luigi, feeling tears sting my eyes. As though sensing my distress, Agostino brushed along the sides of my body in a way that soothed me all too much than I would like to admit. I buried my face in his chest, not wanting to witness such a moment because I knew that it would make me even sadder. In seconds, I heard a shocked grunt, in the silence, followed by a loud thud as Luigi's body fell to the ground.

I risked taking my face out of Agostino's chest to see, and when I did, I found a knife perfectly lodged through his heart, blood escaping as he laid there with his eyes wide open. Looking at the men, they looked just as they did those moments ago, as if none of them had even moved an inch. But I noticed the subtle difference in Paolo's body, as he brought his arm back down to his body. I realised that he must have flung the knife directly into the chest of Luigi.

Agostino walked me around Luigi's body, taking me to Giacomo who would be the one who would walk me down the aisle.

I walked out of the room, arm in arm with Giacomo, Agostino behind us, but Paolo didn't follow. The door closed behind Agostino as the two men walked as though they had done nothing wrong at all. I felt the dark veil being lifted from behind my hair and then brought up and over my head, completely shielding me from the world.

EPILOGUE

"My, if someone would have told all those years ago…maybe even a little less than a year ago that one of the most powerful women in the underworld would be a black-…African woman, I would have laughed," the wretched voice of the very woman who had raised Agostino said. My fingers tightened around the expensive glass of 1945 Dalmore whisky. I had acquired a taste for scotch whisky- anything really that would make me feel like I was escaping from this new life that demanded so much out of me even though I wanted nothing to do with it. I didn't drink too much though, Agostino wouldn't allow it.

In fact, this was my first drink in weeks, and he only allowed me to drink during special occasions. I wouldn't dare go behind his back and drink, especially since he told me that I had to be sober as much as possible to take care of our infant son. But to be honest, I barely take care of him. Agostino hired 7 nannies who made sure that all of our son's needs were tended to. I was only meant to coddle him whenever he seemed to need me.

In the months that I was staying in Rome with my husband who recently became the Don of the Milano family mafia, and our new-born son- I began to learn a lot about Agostino and his life. I learned that his mother had been a whore that his father used to sleep with- a common Gypsy woman that everyone looked down upon. She only told his father about him after he was born, and his father didn't have the nerve to kill his first and only son- so instead, he took him for himself. He brought Agostino to his older sister- a woman who couldn't have her own children- to raise his son to be a man.

In the little time that I have known her, I see why and how Agostino became the way that he was. She was a wretched woman, who I'm glad never had the pleasure of carrying life because she seemed too at ease with taking it. She despised me, maybe even more than I hated her, because to her I was a low life- way worse than the Gypsy whore who had given birth to Agostino. She never had to say anything because I could just sense it; I could just see it in her eyes when she looked at me. But she wouldn't dare to utter a word or even give me a dirty look- not if she still wanted to see the light of day. Agostino ruled with an iron fist and he had spoken against his family and warned that whoever dared to comment on my skin colour, would pay the price with their family's lives. There were a few who dared to go against him, and they paid a very heavy price judging by the skulls of their loved ones decorating the décor of our Italian manor.

"Isabella," I said with a sigh as I turned to face the woman, looking down at her. She was wheelchair bound because she didn't have both of her legs since they had been cut at the knees.

The reason for that was; she had crossed Agostino's father back when Agostino was a little boy and the siblings had a disagreement, where she gauged his father's eye, and the dad chopped off her leg. The other leg, she lost because of Agostino...a couple of months back when she said something about our son; Arturo. "I see you're feeling better," I commented, looking down at her and how she concealed the lack of legs with a midnight blue ball gown that was bunched and gathered all around the expensive electrical wheelchair. Her dark hair was pulled into a low messy bun and her makeup was done horribly- just the way that she liked. Her blush was too bright, the foundation was cracking, and the Botox that she did only seemed to age her even more.

"Ah well, what can I say, I know my son can be a little sensitive at times," she said with a smile that didn't reach her dark beady eyes that bored into mine brazenly.

"I guess telling Agostino that his son had "ugly negro hair" might have touched a bit of a nerve," I commented with a dry tone even though a chill did run down my spine at the memory of her loud and pained screams as Agostino sliced her leg off with rusted saw. She had cried and begged, screaming in absolute agony and as much as I hated her and absolutely despised her comment about my son's hair- I had begged for her mercy, begging for him to not do more to her than he had already done.

It scared me how he did it so calmly and expertly. I knew that he had earned his dono della morte name, however it didn't make it any less terrifying to see him do that to someone who raised him. He had begun with her toes, pulling each one off with a plier, before he went to her foot and sawed it off at the ankle; then he got up, made some food and left her out there all night before he returned the next morning and sawed off her leg at the knee.

Her eyes looked me down and up, taking in my attire for tonight's "charity" event where some of Italy's most powerful were present. I say "charity" event because that was the cover of this evening, however we all knew that business deals were going down. Agostino was bribing the president of Italy with money that he would be a fool to turn down, he was speaking to ministers about ways to illegally trade and have nothing happen to the business. There were talks on who would be killed next; and the night would end on a high note, with drunken dancing and singing. If there was one thing you could commend Agostino and I on; was our party throwing skills. I guess I tried so hard to keep myself occupied, that I jumped at chances where we could host. I would go all out when it came to décor, entertainment, food, whatever it be that was needed.

"You look nice," she said bitterly, and I looked down at the gown before I smoothed my hand over the $25 million dollar diamond necklace around my neck that went perfectly with the Gray satin and heavily beaded evening gown with long dramatic sleeves that pooled around me. The dress had a sweetheart neckline that showed off the expensive diamond necklace, and the dress revealed the perfect amount of the top of my breasts. It hugged me tight, shaping my body that had managed to bounce back after giving birth and I was back to a more fulfilling body type that I was confident in. The dress was long and dragged far behind me, shielding the expensive custom Jimmy Choo high heels that went perfectly with the dress. My ginger hair was made curly and dramatic, framing my face that was done meticulously with Dior makeup products that enhanced my features and made me look like a dream.

I caught the compelling eyes that belonged to my husband-catching him watching me from across the room, as he always did. I smiled at him and he smiled back after what felt like an eternity, as though he was lost in the very essence of me. The way that Agostino looked at me, it scared me even now. He looked at me as though I was the only person he ever saw, as though I was only person he actually saw as a human and it seemed to confuse him. "the way that he looks at you..." Isabella spoke up and I looked at her, having forgotten that she was even there, "it makes him vulnerable...weak, because he can't hide that you're a living embodiment of his heart and soul." Isabella said, sounding disappointed more than anything.

I cleared my throat and downed the rest of my drink. As soon as I took the final sip, a waitress collected my glass and stepped away. "how is my grandson?" I don't think Isabella cared at all for him.

"Don't pretend like you care, Isabella. You're a wretched and evil and vile woman who deserves to spend the rest of her miserable life strapped to an electrical wheelchair that I hope someday malfunctions and just drives you straight into oncoming traffic." She began to laugh, clearly not hurt at all by what I said.

"You know, I miss the way that things used to be. Look around this meticulous ball room and everyone here? Are you seeing what I'm seeing? There's no one in here like you," she said with an ugly snarl. "this life is meant for people like us, the life of luxury, wealth and power, its meant for us, pure bloods. Not for..."

she didn't have to say the words because I knew exactly what she meant. "you're out of your element, my beloved daughter in law."

I turned my head to look down at her before I bent over until she and I were at eye level. "don't look around this room, Isabella, look into my eyes. Make sure you take me in and take in everything that I say. I don't care about how things used to be. I don't care that you were sleeping with your own father and earned the curse of being barren by your mother as consequence of you being one sick bitch," I said calmly, "it's really so sad, so sad how your life has turned out, Isabella. You're right.

As I look around this room, I see everything that you wished to have. I see the luxury that you wish was yours, the power that you wish you had coursing through your veins. But now you just have to sit back and watch a black African bitch run the show and it makes your blood boil." I leaned in even closer, making it a point to touch her pearl necklace and adjust it neatly, "listen to me, and listen to me carefully, Isabella, you will never be me, you will never take my place, and that 'son' of yours," I nodded in the direction of Agostino with a ghost of a smile on my face, "he's eight inches deep inside of me every night, so pussy whipped that your life lies in my hands.

So I suggest you never disrespect me, your superior, or my son ever again, or I will have dono della morte take you down to his basement." I straightened up and clicked my fingers, a waitress appearing with a tray of drinks, "have a lovely night Isabella, it was great seeing you." I said with a smile as I took a glass of whisky and walked away.

I walked towards Agostino who noticed me coming and straightened up, placing an empty glass of whisky on a silver tray. He extended his arm and pulled me into his body when I was close enough before he leaned down and placed a kiss to my lips, "should I end her life, my dear Autumn dove?" he asked me, as though he was simply waiting for the order. Of course, Agostino was aware of everything and was probably just watching the situation between his 'mother' and I.

I shook my head and placed my hand on his chest, playing with his tie, "I just want to see my baby. Take me to our son." He didn't need to be told twice because he placed my hand in the crook of his arm and we began to walk out of the ballroom and towards the other wing of the home, that would take us to Arturo's wing. I let out a hearty sigh as we walked into his bedroom and Agostino closed the door behind us while I approached Arturo's crib. I watched him lay there peacefully, asleep in his baby blue onesie. I ran my finger along his tiny face as I stared at him like it was my first time seeing him.

"Look at him..." I said, my heart filling with joy and love in a way that I never knew would be possible, "he's so pure...so beautiful."

Agostino was silent for a moment before he spoke up, "I am building an empire for him to take over. He will continue my legacy, reach lengths that I won't be able to reach, and it will have all been possible because of you," Agostino placed a kiss to my cheek as I still at his words and nervously swallowed because I didn't want that to be the future of our son. I didn't want his future to be something of darkness and bloodshed. "we have a bright future ahead of us, my Autumn dove, and any future with you in it is far beyond my wildest dreams.

My dear, my love, my Autumn dove, you have made me the man that I am today, will make the man that I will be tomorrow, and mould the man that I will be in the future. Together, we can do anything, we can take over the world, step by step." He turned me around and made me face him, his eyes taking me in, the hunger that he has for me and my body showing so clearly on his face, "no one, and I mean no one, will ever take you away from me. I will never let you go..."

9 781944 253387